LETHAL SALVATION
SHADOW ELITE BOOK FIVE

ARC COPY ONLY

MADDIE WADE

Lethal Salvation
Shadow Elite Book Five
By Maddie Wade

Published by Maddie Wade
Copyright © November 2022

Cover: Clem Parsons-Metatec
Editing: Black Opal Editing
Formatting: Black Opal Editing

This is a work of fiction. Names characters places and incidents are a product of the author's imagination or are used fictitiously and are not to be construed as fact. Any resemblance to actual events organisations or persons—living or dead—is entirely coincidental.

All rights reserved. By payment of the required fees, you have been granted the non-exclusive non-transferable right to access and read the text of this eBook on a screen. Except for use in reviews promotional posts or similar uses no part of this text may be reproduced transmitted downloaded decompiled reverse-engineered or stored in or introduced into any information storage and retrieval system in any form or by any means whether electronic or mechanical now known or hereafter invented without the express written permission of the author.

First edition November 2022 ©Maddie Wade

Acknowledgments

I am so lucky to have such an amazing team around me without which I could never bring my books to life. I am so grateful to have you in my life, you are more than friends you are so essential to my life.

My wonderful beta team, Greta, and Deanna who are brutally honest and beautifully kind. If it is rubbish you tell me, it is and if you love it you are effusive. Your support means so much to me.

My editing team—Linda and Dee at Black Opal Editing. Linda is so patient, she is so much more than an editor, she is a teacher and friend.

Thank you to my group Maddie's Minxes, your support and love for Fortis, Eidolon, Ryoshi and now Shadow Elite you are so important to me. Special thanks to Rowena, Tracey, Faith, Rachel, Carolyn, Kellie, Maria, Rochelle, Becky, Vicky, Greta, Deanna, Sharon and Linda L for making the group such a friendly place to be.

My UK PA Clem Parsons who listens to all my ramblings and helps me every single day.

My ARC Team for not keeping me on edge too long while I wait for feedback.

Lastly and most importantly thank you to my readers who have embraced my books so wholeheartedly and shown a love for the stories in my head. To hear you say that you see my characters as family makes me so humble and proud. I hope you enjoy Duchess and Gideon's love story as much as I did.

Cover: Clem Parsons @Metatec
Editing: Black Opal Editing

To everyone who has ever loved a bad boy in a suit.

PROLOGUE

"What do you mean, they won't help him?"

Nadia, known as Duchess to all who met her, faced down her boss, hands on her hips and her temper simmering just below the surface.

Frank Beasley looked up at her from his desk and sighed as he ran his hand through his barely existent hair. "Like I said, Hadi can claim asylum, but the British Government won't finance his relocation to the UK."

Rolling her lips between her teeth, she tried to control the fury that bubbled. Showing emotion was something she'd worked hard on in her role at MI6. Being half Italian, she'd inherited her mother's temper and looks, and her father's love of languages. It was the love of language that had gotten her this job but now it was her Italian ancestry that was screaming to the forefront. "So, let me get this straight. Hadi risks his life for the UK government and people, and now we're just going to abandon him and his family? This is bullshit, Frank."

"Listen, Duchess, I don't disagree but my hands are tied."

"Bullshit. You've done shadier shit than this and pulled harder strings. You just don't want to."

Frank eyed her, his normally passive emotionless face going hard. "Watch yourself, Duchess. You're already on thin ice after that last job."

"Oh, you mean the one where I rescued a pregnant mother from being raped by one of those assholes on the base?"

"You put him in the hospital for five weeks."

"Asshole is lucky that's all I did."

"He was a fucking ally."

"Not to me and not to women. He was scum and you know it."

"I'm not doing this with you, Duchess. They said no, end of story."

"No."

Frank leaned back in his chair as she looked down at him, wondering how the hell he ever got this job and then realising it was because he was a yes man. Something she'd never be, could never be. It was standing there she came to the realisation that after six years at MI6 perhaps her time was coming to an end. She loved the work and her people, but the red tape and politics weren't for her.

She'd thought she could help people and use her gift of languages at the same time and, for a time, she had, but now she was seeing more and more that for every person she helped, there were ten more that they couldn't. All because of bureaucracy and keeping the peace so some little dickhead in Whitehall or the Pentagon didn't get their knickers in a twist.

"No?"

"Yes, Frank." She leaned forward. "No. If you won't help him, I will."

His face went an interesting shade of red, one of her favourite colours usually as he stood to face her, trying to use his height to intimidate her. It wouldn't work. She might be of average height and build but she was trained by the best of the best. A bonus of working so close with the UK special forces was that she got to train with them and learn from the most skilled operators in the world.

"If you go against me on this, Duchess, I'll fire your ass."

She could see the bluff beneath the bluster and wondered again how he could possibly have gotten to this position before she remembered that he might be a weasel, but he was a cunning one too.

"Fine. I quit."

She could see the tiny capillaries in his cheeks almost burst from anger and she wanted to laugh.

"You don't just quit MI6, Duchess."

"Watch me."

Duchess spun on her heel and walked to the door, before turning around and dropping the calm façade, letting him see the operative who'd taken down four gunmen singlehandedly while nursing a knife wound in her side. "A word to the wise, Frank. You go up against me and you'll regret it."

He huffed and rolled his eyes, but the slight intake of air gave away his unease.

"What could you possibly do to me, Duchess?"

"Oh, I don't know. Maybe make sure the powers that be know that you were the reason that asset was captured by the Russians, or maybe how that intel you sent to Red Team wasn't checked as you assured them it was and that was why they lost a good man."

His jaw ticked and she found it fascinating to watch him squirm and try and decide if she had what it took. She had and she did, and she absolutely would take this man down if he crossed her.

"Get out of here, Duchess, and let's see how long you last on your own."

"Oh, I'll be fine. After all, you were the one who taught me that in MI6, we're all on our own in the end."

Turning on her heel, she walked out of the room, down the stairs, and out the back door of 85 Albert Embankment. Crossing the road, she walked along the bank of the River Thames, noting the people strolling along with little awareness of how lucky they were to be free. A smile twitched at the corners of her mouth, and she felt a weight lift off her shoulders. She hadn't realised how stifling it had been working for MI6 and how badly she'd needed to walk away until she'd done it.

It had been a spur-of-the-moment decision but that was her. She made choices in the moment, and they'd not let her down so far. Duchess trusted her gut above all else and it had been telling her for months that something was wrong, and now she knew it was this.

Looking over her shoulder, she spotted a guy in a grey jacket as one of the younger, newer recruits. Duchess knew Frank would have someone following her, checking on her and reporting back about what she was doing, and she didn't care. If she wanted to lose this person, they'd believe she was a wraith with how well she could smoke them.

Slipping into a café, she ordered a large latte with vanilla syrup and two slices of tiffin. The sweet treat was her weakness and something she only indulged in on rare occasions, but today she felt like celebrating. Today was a win before she got to the job of planning what the hell she'd do with her life next. Luckily, her savings would get her through at least a year, but she didn't want that time without a focus; she needed to keep busy. She'd start with a plan to help get her friend Hadi and his family out of Afghanistan.

Generous, kind Hadi and his sweet wife, who'd welcomed her into their home, knowing the risks they were taking by working for the British Army as interpreters and still doing it. Fury prickled her skin as she paid for the coffee and sweets and left. They'd been thrown away like left over takeout and she hated it. The walk to her apartment was short as she slipped through side streets and nipped between traffic until she was in a quieter part of Vauxhall. Her apartment was small, barely big enough to swing a cat, not that she was there very often. Stopping at the door, she turned and clocked her new shadow and gave him a wave, watching as he went slack-jawed and cursed before spinning on his heel and walking away. He wouldn't go far, she knew. He'd radio in and then swap out with another person to tail her.

It didn't matter, she was in for the night now. She had work to do and favours to call in from one very particular person.

∼

THE BUZZ of the needle on her skin settled her in a way nothing else could. The slight tingle of pain, the smell of the ink, and the low music the artist was playing were all just background as Duchess let the stress and strain of the last few weeks leave her body.

Hadi and his family were safe and that was all that she cared about. Closing her eyes, she let her mind drift over the possibilities for her future. She could go and see her mother in Italy for a few weeks or travel to all the places she kept promising herself she'd go back to as a tourist, and not as an undercover MI6 operative.

Venice, the Philippines, Republic of Congo were such beautiful sites. Some were mired in war you could see, some in a war that nobody realised was happening, buried beneath the veneer of tourism and smiles.

Her body sensed him before her mind, everything tensing as the tattoo artist lifted his needle from her skin. Duchess flattened her hand to the side of her leg to the knife she had hidden beneath the folds of the long, flowy summer dress.

He was to her left, an energy around him that she knew so well because it flowed through her own veins. Spy or something else she couldn't quite tell but he was dangerous, so much so that her gut was screaming.

Poised and ready to strike, she sat up abruptly, her movements fluid and fast, the knife biting into the soft skin of his throat before she registered who it was. Their eyes locked, her jaw hardening before she grinned. "You're slipping, Jack."

Jack Granger, the man, the myth, the legend. He'd been her contact when she'd worked abroad. His unit was the one who'd taught her these moves, made sure she was safe and could defend herself properly. He and his men had made her more than the SIS ever could.

He smiled and she wondered how it could be possible that this man did nothing for her in a sexual way. He was drop dead, panty-melting hot, women literally fell at his feet and yet he and she had never had that between them. He was like a brother to her, or a cousin at the least.

"It's good to see you, Duchess."

Cocking her head, she regarded him thoughtfully. "I have to say I wasn't expecting a visit so soon."

Jack pulled the chair the tattoo artist had been using closer and sat, his hands clasped loose between his thighs, before turning to the man who was watching them, the tattoo gun in his hand and a bored look on his face.

"Can you give us a few minutes in private, Jerry?"

Her smile and request were met with a wink. Jerry was covered head to toe in ink and looked like he ate small children for breakfast and yet he was the most devoted family man she knew of.

"Sure, Duchess, but don't go messing up my studio."

"We won't, I promise. This is a friend."

Jerry eyed Jack and shook his head. "You lot are weird."

She wondered if he saw the irony in his words as he left, closing the door behind him and leaving them in peace.

Her focus found Jack again and she quirked a brow. "Well?"

"I have a proposition for you."

"Oh?"

"I'm setting up a team and I want you to be second in command of it."

Her interest was piqued. She hadn't expected this and was intrigued. Jack never did anything by halves. After leaving the SAS, he could have gone in so many different directions, but he'd set up Eidolon and gone on to be the Queen's personal protection and all-round royal clean-up crew. They took their orders from her and cleaned up messes left by her government or in some cases jobs that just felt personal to her and them.

"I'm listening."

His lips twitched. "This team will be completely off the books. For all intents and purposes, it won't exist. You'll answer to me, but there'll also be a certain amount of autonomy."

"What kind of jobs?"

"Since the royal tour, we've become more 'seen', for want of a better word. Eidolon must be more careful in what we take on."

Duchess felt an excitement begin to trickle through her veins, a knowledge that this was a pivotal moment for her in some way. "So, this new team would take them on?"

"Yes. Eidolon will obviously still do what we do, but some of the hotter, dirtier jobs will be for the new team."

"What kind of operators and how many?"

"I was thinking ten or twelve to start and a mix of operators. What I've found is there's a certain contingent of society that's being overlooked."

"I don't disagree but who specifically?"

"The grey people."

Duchess felt herself smile at his words; she knew exactly who he meant but wanted confirmation. "Explain?"

"Those people who are connected and skilled but perhaps morally considered a bit grey, or technically would end up in prison for their crimes, when the truth is, their pasts aren't black and white. Then there are the ones who've been fucked over by the systems they work within, and their skills are about to go to waste or end up used for things not worthy of them."

"Sounds like a ragtag bunch."

"Yes, but an elite ragtag bunch nonetheless."

"And you want me to lead them with someone else?"

"Yes."

"Why me?"

"Come on, Duchess. You were running the section, not Frank. Everyone knew it, except him. You're a natural leader."

"So are a lot of people."

"Maybe, but you also have integrity, and you trust your gut. You're calm and controlled, but not afraid to ruffle feathers and kick asses when you need to."

She was all those things, but it was nice for someone she respected so highly to see it too. A warm feeling crept in to sink beside the excitement. "Who would be in charge?"

"Niall O'Scanlan, but you know him as Bás."

Duchess drew in a sharp breath, her lungs seizing in shock for a second. "I'm sorry, I thought you said Bás."

Jack kept her gaze, his features coolly blank of emotion. "I did."

"He's a ghost, Jack, and what's more, he's a lone wolf. He doesn't work with anyone, at least not by choice. Nobody even knows who he works for."

"I do and we've worked with him."

Duchess blew out a breath and sat back, a little taken aback by this development. "Wow, I'm not sure what to think about that." Looking up she tried to read him and failed. "Has he agreed?"

"He has but only if you're his second."

"What!" Her screeched word was unlike her, her usual calm failing her as she tried to battle these revelations and put them into some kind of order. "I've never even worked with him. We met once and I told him he was a dick."

Jack leaned forward, his elbows falling to his knees. "Do you know how many people have said that to Bás and lived?"

"No clue."

"One. You. He was a dick and you called him out on it, even knowing who he was, and you didn't buy into his legend or kiss his ass. That's what a man like Bás needs beside him to lead a team of misfits. He's a hot-headed asshole and you balance that out and he knows it."

"So why ask him to lead it, if he's such a loose cannon?"

"I didn't say he was a loose cannon. He's the king of misfits, which is why he'll know exactly how to lead them, but he needs you."

"And he said he won't do it if I don't?"

Jack nodded. "Exactly."

"Shit. This is a lot to take in when I only came in for some ink."

"I know and I hate to be an asshole, but the offer ends when I walk out this room."

"You love being an asshole, Jack, so don't lie." Her words were coated with a smile as she rubbed her hands over the cotton of her long summer dress.

"Yeah, maybe."

"So, tell me more about how it would work?"

"I have an idea for a base of operations, which would be totally secure, with living quarters and a command centre. Those that want to live close could if they so choose, but secrecy is key. We'd have a front of some kind for the locals and any other nosey parkers so we can come and go as we please. Some of the team members may choose to go completely off the grid and any record of them will be wiped, their deaths staged if they want, but that's not imperative. If you think MI6 was top secret, this is more so. Nobody can know about this team but those I choose to tell and her Majesty. Pay will be negotiated but let's just say you'll be able to upgrade your flat if you decide to keep it."

"I can work with that. What about the team, who chooses them?"

"Me, you, and Bás."

Duchess ran the idea over in her mind, coming at it from different angles but since the second Jack had interrupted her tattoo, she'd known her answer. Sticking out her hand. "You've got yourself a second in command."

Jack smiled wide and it was so unusual she almost felt a flutter of attraction. "One condition."

"Name it."

"I get to choose the team's name."

"Fine with me."

"Now, can I finish my tattoo?"

"Sure. I'll wait at the café on the corner you like so much."

"Why?" Duchess was puzzled.

"We have a team to pick and Bás is waiting."

Duchess clenched her jaw and raised her eyebrow at him. "Really? You were so sure I'd say yes?"

"More like, quietly confident."

"Asshole."

Jack's deep chuckle rang out as he disappeared through the door, and she sat back and waited for Jerry to come back in and finish the sleeve of peonies on her arm. It was her last sitting for this one and she wanted to get it done today. Jack and Bás would have to wait for her. After all, a Duchess never bowed to any man.

CHAPTER 1

"Good morning, Mr Cavendish, here are your papers for the day."

Duchess handed Damon Cavendish the papers as she did every morning since she'd gone undercover as his secretary. Her role was to get more dirt on Carter Cavendish and his mother, Marsha.

Damon looked up at her with his usual smile missing from his face. "Thank you."

"What's wrong?"

"We have a meeting in the boardroom in five minutes."

He looked annoyed and instantly Duchess went on alert. "There's nothing in the diary, Mr Cavendish." Keeping up appearances for the other staff was imperative to her cover, so she bowed and scraped when others were within hearing distance, as was expected of a corporate secretary. They were, she was finding out, the real power in these towers of industry. They held the keys to the kingdom and yet were made to act as if the only thing of interest was between their legs, not their ears. Her respect for them had tripled during this stint and so had her admiration because anticipating a man's every need, from his dry cleaning to his corporate calendar and every minute in between, was hard work, but she grudgingly admitted she had enjoyed parts of it.

Damon glanced around the outer sanctum of his office space, which had been her home for six months. "My brother called it last minute."

"I see. Will I be needed?"

"Yes."

His tone was flat and unimpressed as Damon went into his office and closed the door on her, leaving her to wonder what the hell was going on, and more importantly, why did Damon look so pissed off. He was usually calm, friendly, and would stop to chat and flirt with her, despite their relationship being one of friendship.

The three Cavendish brothers were very different, yet all had the same gorgeous dark looks and sexy build.

Carter was the half-sibling to Gideon and Damon, having a different mother. He was the man she was after, who she knew was involved in Project Cradle. He ran an illegal billion-pound empire of drugs, human trafficking, guns, and any other manner of dirty disgusting things, using the family business of Cavendish Enterprises and their ownership of casinos, hotels, and respected fashion houses to hide his activities. It was why she was there. The older two brothers wanted no part of it but their father was a man who had his testicles firmly in the palm of his wife and she controlled him and gave their son Carter whatever he wanted, including letting him use Cavendish as a front.

Damon was the front man, or the face of Cavendish Enterprises, who attended the galas and events. He dated beautiful women, charmed investors, and was an astute and well-respected barrister who handled a lot of pro-bono work. He was a good man and had become a solid friend to her as they'd worked together to take down Carter and remove the stink from the Cavendish empire once and for all.

Then there was Gideon, gorgeous, sexy, grumpy, aloof, and cold. He was a business genius and there wasn't a deal in this city that went down without his knowledge. He was the reason the legal side of the business was becoming more successful than the illegal side. He was the man she hated with a passion and wanted with a desperation she couldn't fathom. He plagued her nightmares and her dreams in equal measure.

He was the man who could get her killed because he was distracting and dangerous to her equilibrium. Which was why she worked for Damon on this project. Both Damon and Gideon knew why she was really there and wanted Shadow's help to take down their half-brother, blood in this case was not thicker than water, and there was no love lost between the older brothers and Carter. Duchess wasn't a fool though, she knew working alongside Gideon, a man who could make her forget who she was would be a disaster, hence Damon was her 'boss'.

"Time to go."

She'd been so deep in thought that she hadn't heard Damon approach. She jumped up and raced after him. Just another example of how distracting any thought of Gideon could be.

Her skin itched from the make-up she wore to hide her tattoos in the stuffy corporate environment, but she couldn't afford for her ink, which she was proud of, to draw attention she didn't need. Mousy, plain, and forgettable was what she was going for in a knee-length black skirt and a high-neck white blouse, flawless skin meant she could get away with little make-up, and red lips were her only nod to her real self.

Her dark hair was in a tight bun at the base of her neck, which gave her a raging headache by the day's end. It was so far from the real her as to be laughable, but a great cover.

Entering the large conference room, she saw it was empty. The glass table held enough seats for every board member and overlooked the Canary Wharf in London's business district. The view was beautiful, even on a dreary day like today. As she gazed across the expanse of London, she found her eyes drawn to the Embankment and her mind flitted to her time at MI6. So much had changed for her. Shadow made a difference to people without the bullshit of politics getting involved, but she knew to erase the poison of greed and evil in the world they would need a thousand teams like Shadow.

Pulling her mind back into the present, she rounded on her fake boss, hands on hips. "What's going on, Damon?"

"What's going on is that there's going to be a slight shake-up in personnel."

Duchess turned to see Gideon stalking toward her like a slow loose-limbed predator about to take a bite out of some poor unsuspecting deer. She had a feeling he thought she was the deer in this scenario, poor misguided man. He wore a handmade Italian three-piece suit in charcoal grey, a hand-stitched dark blue shirt, and a black tie, which probably cost more than her weekly food bill. He looked deadly, dangerous, sexy as hell, and her body wanted to swoon at the sight of him, but Duchess wasn't going to let him see the effect he had on her body, not if she could help it.

Straightening her spine, she ignored her erect nipples and hoped he wouldn't notice, refusing to give in to the desire to cross her arms over her chest and look weak.

He glanced down and smirked before brushing past her, the arm of his suit grazing her shoulder and causing a frisson of lust to shoot through her body.

"Damon, I need a PA. Mine quit and, as you're in court for the next six weeks or so, I'd like Miss Benassi to stand in until I can arrange someone more suitable."

Damon glanced at her and she glared at him, daring him to agree. He shrugged and turned to his brother. "It's not up to me, is it? You know the score, brother. Nadia doesn't work for us, not really." Damon was the only one who called her Nadia, to Gideon it was always Miss Benassi.

"Then that's settled. Miss Benassi, please move your belonging to my office immediately."

Gideon spun as if to leave and she lost her cool. "I don't think so.

I'm here to do a job and you know for a fact that's not to be your Girl Friday."

Gideon pinned her with a glare as he strode toward her, stopping mere centimetres from her. Her heart rate licked up and it was almost impossible to stop the way his angry gaze shot straight to her pussy. She could smell his aftershave, something spicy that reminded her of sweaty sex and champagne. Images conjured in her mind of them fucking, fighting for dominance as each took and took from the other, until there was nothing left.

He looked down at her, even in her four-inch heels she could not match his six-foot-four height. "I'm quite aware of why you are here."

"Then you know I'm perfectly fine where I am."

"On the contrary, Miss Benassi. You need access to Carter, and I need a PA. If I don't get that, you'll no longer have our help in this matter."

Bastard. He was playing games, expecting her to cave and beg for his help. He had no clue who he was dealing with.

"Gideon! Don't be rash. We need her."

Gideon held up his hand to his brother, who swore. "We do not need her, but I'll agree she is helpful and somewhat nice to look at."

Damon threw up his hands and walked toward the door of the conference room, about to leave her alone to deal with the devil.

Gideon's gaze swept over her body making it clear what he thought her uses were. This arrogant prick was pushing her buttons, trying to get a reaction. Well, she'd give him one. "It's fine, Damon. I can work with Gideon for six weeks, but I have my own terms."

Her friend held her eyes a moment longer trying to read her, before he nodded, satisfied with what he saw and left the room.

Gideon's eyes flickered as they dropped to her lips. "What would those be?"

"I want more access to Carter. I want to be seen at the galas, the dinners. I want to know everything about his habits outside of work and I want to see him interact with his mother and your father."

"Done." Gideon smiled and it looked more like a threat than a happy emotion. "Please find a more appropriate work wardrobe, Miss Benassi. I can see your nipples through that blouse."

With that, he turned and left the conference room, and she fought the urge to go after him and show him just how much he'd under-estimated her. A smile spread over her lips as she thought of all the things she'd do to make him pay for his arrogance. She'd seen the want in his eyes, the desire for her, but she wouldn't get sucked into his dicksand. He was a man who wanted control, to dominate and dictate. Unfortunately for him, she was the same way. The only difference between them was the fact she saw him for what he was, and he had no clue who he was dealing with, but he was about to find out.

CHAPTER 2

Throwing his pen across the desk, Gideon let out a breath of frustration. One hundred and twenty-eight minutes, that's how long she'd been occupying the desk outside his office and he hadn't got a lick of work done in that time. She was costing him money and, more importantly, time, distracting him with her sexy buttoned-up blouses and tight skirts.

Since the moment he'd laid eyes on Nadia Benassi, he'd fought the urge to either strangle her or bend her over his desk and slide his cock inside her. He'd thought the myriad of dirty, illicit fantasises running through his brain would settle when he had her working as his temporary PA. Gideon had a strict rule about fucking the staff and placing her in that position put her off limits. The problem was his dick hadn't got the memo, apparently.

Work and pleasure were kept separate. He had no desire to end up on his brother's docket in court for a sexual harassment charge. Having Nadia as his PA seemed like the perfect plan to calm his dick into submission, but it hadn't worked. He was hard as stone, horny as a fucking teenager, and out of control in a way he hated.

His stomach growled and he lifted his head to the door feeling irritated and annoyed and there was only one person responsible. Pushing back his chair so hard it almost hit the window behind him, he adjusted his cock in his trousers and stalked to the door. Yanking it open, he found the object of his irritation holding court outside his door, her desk surrounded by other staff members from the executive floor. She was like a flame drawing all these little moths to her brightness.

A sexy little blonde with a too-short skirt spotted him first and her face went to twist into a smile. He frowned, giving her a look that he knew would quell her advances instantly. Her face dropped, her skin going paler before she turned and fled. Gideon watched her hurry back to her desk, never looking behind her to see if the others followed. The other two women, one from finance and the other he had no idea about, followed suit.

"What the hell is going on here?"

Nadia tipped her head up to him, her long elegant neck arching and regal, her shoulders and back straight as he let his gaze move over her form. Her body was downright fucking sinful, and although he'd called her out for her attire like a dick earlier, she was dressed perfectly appropriately for the office. The problem was a body like that didn't belong in an office, it belonged spread out on his bed.

She had long, toned legs, perfect slim ankles showing good breeding, and a curvy ass he envisioned grabbing with both hands as he fucked into her from behind. A slim waist, gorgeous tits that would spill out of his hands, and then a delicate collar bone revealing her graceful neck. In a world that was fair, she'd at least be ugly, have a broken curved nose or yellow teeth, but no, she was utter perfection.

High cheek bones, full luscious red lips he'd imagined wrapped around his cock a thousand times over and the most unique hazel eyes that seemed to switch to green depending on her mood. It all made him exceedingly frustrated because he wanted her badly, but when she opened her mouth, he just wanted to tan her ass and put her in her place. She was confrontational and snippy, something he hated in a woman. He just needed his libido to get the message.

"I'm having my lunch break."

His temper ratcheted up now as he stalked closer, pulled by some invisible string. "How nice for you, and who gave you permission?"

Her eyes narrowed and he could see her trying to fight her instinct to fight with him. In a perverse way, he hoped she did fight him. He liked fight in a woman, some backbone and steel. He was distinctly disappointed when she schooled her expression so he couldn't read it.

"Of course, Mr Cavendish. I apologise." She pushed her half-eaten sandwich into her desk drawer and turned back to him. "What can I do for you."

Something about her submitting made a hollow place in his belly. He didn't like it, so he went on the offensive. "Get me the reports on the Macey deal, book me a table at Pier One for tonight, and don't forget my lunch." He gave her drawer a heated look of annoyance.

"Yes of course. What would you like for lunch?"

He sighed and rubbed his temple and looked away from her, not trusting himself to not let his gaze wander to her tits again. "Whole wheat Italian bread with chicken and salad, and make sure it's organic. I don't want any of that processed shit poisoning my body."

He thought he heard her mutter something under her breath but when his eyes flashed to her face, she was merely looking at him waiting for him to answer.

"You need to learn to satisfy my needs quickly, Miss Benassi. I don't have the time to train you and hold your hand like a goddamn babysitter. I'm demanding and if you can't handle that, I suggest you pack your shit and leave."

He was pushing her; he knew it and so did she. Gideon wasn't even sure if he wanted her to tell him to stick his job up his ass and the chance at catching Carter with it or if he wanted her to stay and keep delivering this torture on a daily basis.

He saw her eyes flicker, a fire growing beneath the calm façade she was showing the world. He had the sudden urge to peel back each layer until she was nothing but heat and passion. As quickly as it came, it was smoothed away as if he'd never glimpsed it.

"Absolutely, Mr Cavendish. Is there anything else?"

The capitulation made his stomach settle but did nothing to ease the ache in his balls. "No."

He turned on his heel and walked back to his office, slamming the door so hard it rattled the hinges and feeling more unsettled and gnarly than when he went out there. He fought the urge to reach up and loosen his tie. Showing a weakness by looking rattled to anyone was a mistake he'd learned at a young age, and letting her see him ruffled was a weakness.

Head down, he opened his emails and saw the Macey reports in his inbox with the time stamp thirty minutes ago. He wondered why she hadn't told him she'd sent them over already. Perhaps she wanted him on the back foot. For him to feel contrite but he didn't. She was there to do the work of PA as her cover, and she damn well better learn that he required, no demanded, utter perfection from his staff and executed the same level of discipline for himself.

He kept his head down, ignoring her when she delivered his lunch, not even saying thank you. It was how he'd be with anyone else, and he was resolved to act the same way with her.

By late afternoon, he'd finally got his head into work. The Macey contract was huge, a fashion house they'd been coveting for years and would finally give them the foothold in the US that they wanted.

What he didn't like was the email he got from Carter asking for him to send over the financials for the take-over plan. Nothing good would ever come from Carter or his mother, Marsha, poking their noses in where it wasn't wanted. This side, his side, of the business was clean, and he was killing himself trying to distance himself from the shady side.

His father marrying Marsha when he and Damon were eight and ten was when their family, and more importantly his father, began to change. Up until then their father, if not exactly winning any father of the year awards, was at least present and showed an interest in them.

Marsha had quickly had him and his brother shipped off to boarding school, which at the time he'd been glad of. He didn't like her from the start and her cool looks and belittling comments, passed off as innocent observations and caring, even at the age of ten, had been clear to him. Damon, however, had hated boarding school and taken a long time to adjust. He'd been close to their mother and missed her terribly.

After that, it was home for holidays only and when Carter came along, they'd been made to feel even more as if they were unwanted strangers in their own home. The golden child had been worshipped by Marsha and his father.

Only when he'd finished his master's in business had his father shown a renewed interest and pulled him into the business, handing off more and more of the reins to him so he could play golf or jet off on yet another holiday with Marsha. It was then Gideon had seen the real damage being done to his family's legacy. Bad deals and business arrangements that didn't sit well, or with people Gideon knew weren't the kind of organisations they should be involved with. It only got worse when Carter got involved.

Gideon brushed his fingers through his dark hair, yanking at the ends in frustration. He needed Carter dealt with. His mind went to the little boy he'd been and for a while he'd been sweet, looking up to him and Damon but it had changed when he was about ten. Carter had become jealous, demanding, spoiled, and Marsha had indulged his every whim.

His father by that point had checked out and let them do what they wanted. A quiet life seemed more important than being a real parent to his sons. When Carter insisted on being involved with the business, Gideon and Damon flat-out refused. Carter was clever but he was lazy and lacked the work ethic needed to run an empire.

However, Marsha had gotten involved and before he knew it, his father had demanded he give Carter a place in the company, or he'd take Gideon's position as CEO and have the board remove him and install Carter. He knew he could never allow his brother to run this company, so he'd agreed, feeling some control was better than none.

At least he'd thought that until he realised how badly Carter was dragging them into the dark, illicit world of illegal gambling, drugs, prostitution, and God knew what else. The call from Eidolon revealing just how bad things were had been the final straw for him and Damon and they'd agreed to work with the organisation in secret to take down Carter and Marsha. His only fear was his father would be caught in the web too. He'd had to lock that doubt away though because he'd tried to warn his dad. He and Damon both had and, while he understood it was difficult for him to choose one son over another, he had done exactly that and chosen wrong. He'd have to step up and pay for that mistake.

A laugh rang out, husky and sexy and he looked up at his closed door sharply. What the hell was going on now? Standing, he ran his hands through his hair to smooth the frayed ends and then adjusted his cuffs before opening the door.

Unjustified rage and jealousy shot through him as he took in the scene in front of him. Tom Lockett, his business analyst was sitting on the edge of Nadia's desk, his body curved towards her, a smirk on his face as he flirted with her.

Gideon grit his molars so hard he could almost feel them crack as he fought not to react and lash out like he wanted to. Approaching slowly, he knew Nadia had seen him. The woman had instincts like a prey animal, always aware and watching. Tom, however, did not and jumped when he spoke.

"I didn't know I was paying you to flirt with my staff, Tom." He could feel the tension in his jaw as Tom gaped, his lips flapping before he let out a nervous laugh.

"Hey, Gideon, I was just coming to see you."

"And yet here you are flirting with Miss Benassi."

His eyes darted to Nadia who gave nothing away as she watched them, no enjoyment or anger on her face, just observing them and he had the sudden understanding of what a fly under a microscope felt like.

"No, I was just welcoming her to the company."

"Oh, I'm sorry, I didn't know you were in the HR department now. My mistake, I'll just reach out and make sure security is aware."

Only select personal were allowed on this floor and that didn't include low-level staff members unless invited. There were too many confidential memos and reports being left around to have any Tom, Dick, or Harry wandering around.

"No, I'm here to give you my findings from the IT department."

Gideon was getting bored as he held out his hand. "Well?"

"Oh yeah, sure."

Tom handed him the report and he snatched it away without looking at it.

"Do you want to go through it?"

"No." The truth was he probably should, but he was entertaining too many thoughts of strangling the man right now to spend the next hour going over details.

"Oh, okay. I'll just head back down then."

"You do that. And, Tom, if I ever come out here again and find you flirting with my staff, then you will be fired without a reference. Is that understood?"

He tipped his head as Tom went red, from his blond perfectly styled hair to his neck disappearing into his shirt. He wanted to argue, to tell him he was a prick, and he was, but Gideon knew he wouldn't. He was a sycophant like most people on this floor. The only real person to stand up to him was his brother and the cleaner who worked the night shift. Betty was nearing retirement and only did the job to get out of the house. The one time he'd yelled at her, he'd feared he'd be wearing her mop as a hat for a week. She'd cut him down to size in a firm yet motherly way he could hardly remember. They had been firm friends, if you could call it that, ever since.

"Perfectly."

Gideon zoned back into the conversation and watched Tom walk away before turning his gaze back to Miss Benassi, Nadia, Duchess. They all suited her but in different ways. Now she was the Duchess as she glared at him, and he felt his dick swell with need. Fuck, she'd be something in bed, he just knew she'd be a wild one.

"You're a real dick, aren't you?"

Her words were like cold water to his libido. "Excuse me?"

"He was just being friendly and you went all neanderthal on him. I'm surprised you didn't pull out your dick and piss on my leg."

Her lips wrapped around the word made his cock hard, the image of his fist holding her silky hair back so he could watch. The need to punish her for making him hard at work made Gideon step forward, crowding her in her chair. If he hoped for fear or contrition, he was wrong, this woman wasn't afraid of anyone.

"Miss Benassi, if I'm ever in a position where I'm pulling my cock out around you, then it won't be for anything other than to have you on your knees with your mouth open."

The flush on her cheeks was sudden, as was the way her eyes seemed to darken, her tongue coming out to wet her lips as if she could taste him. Then quick as a flash, it was gone as she put a hand on his chest and stood, pushing him back a step.

"Not even if you beg. Now back up before I decide to teach you some manners."

Gideon smirked, usually this fight would turn him off. He liked his women willing, compliant, with just the hint of fire but with her everything was turned on its head, the tables effectively turned.

The thought made him angry, so he retreated, slamming his door for the second time that day and burying himself in work. He needed this shit with Carter done so he could get the delicious Miss Benassi out of his hair for good and go back to his life. In the meantime, perhaps he'd call one of his usual fuck buddies to come over. He'd clearly been too long without sex if she was all he could think about.

Thank fuck if was Friday.

CHAPTER 3

It was weird being in her old flat after all this time, but nice too. She loved her friends at Shadow, and honestly, at this point, they were more family than anything else and that family was expanding fast.

First Bein found Aoife, then Snow and Seb, Reaper and Lucía, and lastly Bishop and Charlie. That would also include babies very soon. Charlie and Snow were expecting around the same time, and there was beautiful little Fleur, who she adored.

It made working on this case feel more isolating. She wasn't, she knew that they were on the same case working it with her, just not so close. Not having the everyday contact that she was used to gave her a feeling of loneliness she couldn't explain, although she knew in her gut that things were coming to a head with this case. It would be over soon, and she was determined those babies wouldn't be born with this hanging over them, tainting the joy their parents should feel.

Charlie and Bishop especially deserved that, to have the pleasure restored that fate had so cruelly destroyed. It would never stop the worry, and she knew no matter what, she couldn't eradicate that, but she could handle this threat for them, and she would.

She just needed to get that asshole Gideon to stop being, well, such an asshole. It didn't help that being around him turned her into a hormone-riddled sex maniac, seeing desire and jealousy where there was none.

Today had been utter torture, but she could cope as long as the reward was big enough.

Her phone buzzing made her glance at the caller ID. She sighed as she answered the video call request. "Hey, Bás. What's up?"

"Why would something be up? Nothing is up, everything is fine."

Something was definitely up. "It was a figure of speech."

"Oh, in that case, forget it."

"I'm about to head out, do you need anything?"

"An update."

"Well, I'm now working directly for Gideon as his PA. He's promised me more access to Carter and Marsha."

"You don't sound happy about that."

Damn Bás and his ability to read people. "No, I'm happy. He's just a little demanding, that's all."

"Well, if anyone can put him in his place it's you, Duchess."

"Oh, don't worry, I will."

"Watchdog found mentions of Macey's in an email thread between Carter and Gideon. What do you know about it?"

"Well, Macey's is a huge fashion house in the US but they're in financial trouble. Gideon is handling a takeover so they can use it as a foothold into the US." Duchess frowned; Carter being involved was unusual. "I'm surprised Carter is involved. Gideon and Damon don't normally let him near anything on this side of the business."

Bás folded his arms. "Watchdog seems to think Gideon was trying to stall or put him off in the conversation he saw."

Duchess sighed. "Which means Carter wants in and Gideon wants him out."

"If Carter wants in, you can bet your ass it isn't for any other reason than expanding his illegal empire."

"I agree. Have Watchdog dig deeper and find out who the players are and if they tie to Macey's in any way."

Bás smirked. "He's already on the case."

Duchess should have known Bás was already one step ahead. "I had an interesting conversation with a man named Tom Lockett today. He's Gideon's business analyst. He let slip that he'd met Carter a few times in his club and the man was, as he put it, a sound guy and offered him a job. It wouldn't surprise me if Carter has spies throughout the company, feeding him information."

Bás frowned. "Wouldn't he already have access to everything?"

"Mostly but Gideon and Damon also keep as much as they can away from him and Marsha, to stop the stink spreading and poisoning the whole thing."

"Yeah, dirt does have a habit of leeching over everything. I'll have Watchdog look into it. Perhaps Charlie can help with that side of things."

"Good. Any news for me?"

Bás shook his head. "Titan and Lotus are still in the US trying to find out what they can on Director Mills. We need to figure out how close Marsha still is to her father."

"You think they've fixed their relationship and are hiding it?"

"Rykov does. He believes Marsha and her dad falling out over Project Cradle was a ruse. She may have gone in voluntarily as a pregnant teenager but, when she came out and changed her name, she stayed involved, that much we do know. Just not what the capacity was. Watchdog found her papers though and it was her father, CIA Director Mills, who signed her papers to go into the facility."

Duchess mused over the news. Watchdog was their tech guru, and there was generally nothing he couldn't uncover or find. "I wonder what happened to her child."

"That's another angle Bein and Snow are chasing down. Marsha and Carter are the key to the other players and the link to Hansen."

Bás had a real hard-on for Hansen. The CIA officer had a beef with Eidolon too, having manipulated two of the women he worked with as a handler into believing he loved them and then selling them out when they were undercover. Those two women were sisters and were now married to Jack Granger and Javier Lopez.

Hansen had a history with Bás, but nobody knew the details and Bás hadn't shared them either. It was his right, but the time was coming for him to be open, as open and honest as everyone else was required to be with them.

"Keep me posted. I'm heading out to Carter's club to see what I can find out."

"Be careful," Bás commented. "I don't like you being alone there after what happened with Charlie."

"Relax, Bás, he thinks I'm Gideon's PA."

"Yeah, but you were there the night we rescued Andrea and Charlie was shot. He could have seen you."

"He would've come for me before now if he knew."

"Maybe, but I don't like it."

"I can take care of myself, Bás."

"I know that," he replied, "but I'm responsible for you. You're too good of an asset to lose, and I don't want to have to tell Jack if you die."

"Oh, delightful."

"You know what I mean. We need you, Duchess."

"Yes, I do. I'll be careful and check in later, okay? Watchdog can monitor my phone if it makes you happier."

"Oh, he already is."

"Of course he is," she said, unsurprised.

"I might send Hurricane down to ghost you just in case."

"Fine, but he needs to keep his distance. I don't want anyone spooked."

"He will. You know he's good at this."

"I know. I trained him."

"See, he's more than good."

"Whatever. I need to go."

Duchess hung up, knowing Hurricane would be in the air within the hour. As a former RAF SF pilot, he flew anything and loved it.

Slipping the knife into the concealed sheath on her thigh, Duchess slid her foot into the black patent stiletto heel and took a last look in the mirror.

Her tattoos were on display tonight and she admired the sleeve of peonies as well as the artwork of ivy and thorns on her opposite shoulder and clavicle. Her neck was a column of waves that seemed to crash over her collar bones and throat.

The tight black bandeau dress rested midthigh and showcased the roses on her left thigh to her knee. It was freeing to not have the make-up covering her skin, hiding the tattoos she loved so much. They were an extension of her and, if she'd had even an ounce of talent in art, she would have made a career as a tattoo artist, but she had no artistic talent whatsoever.

Grabbing her bag, she tossed her long hair over her shoulder and headed out into the night. She'd just do a little snooping and see if she could get any gossip or get a feel for the club Carter owned.

When she arrived the queue to get in was around the corner and at least five people deep. It was a Friday night and London was buzzing with the weekend crowd. Factoring in that it was pay week for most monthly paid employees, the vibe was perfect for her to blend in with them.

Striding towards the front of the line, she put some extra sway in her hips and winked at the bouncer, who smirked back before unhooking the red rope and allowing her entry. She heard the moans behind her but ignored them. It was well known that if you could get beautiful women in a club, the men would follow and throw money at the bar. Duchess was comfortable using her attributes to get what she needed and trained enough to know how to do it without making a scene. Keeping her hair angled so it fell over her face, and her face turned away from the cameras she'd already clocked, she headed for the bar.

The atmosphere was jumping and loud dance music played as throngs of beautiful people swayed and danced pressed together on the dance floor like an erotic pulse, the beat of the music moving them in slow sultry movements.

Duchess leaned past the arm of a slick-dressed suit to order a gin and tonic from the bartender. She wouldn't drink it, but she needed the ruse to allow her to walk around freely and make her look less aware and more like any other drunk woman in this club.

People would notice a stone-cold sober woman, but someone with a drink in her hand acting slightly drunk would be ignored and overlooked as a threat in a way she needed. Loose lips would give her what she wanted in tiny snippets.

Ignoring the lecherous look of the suit, she winked at the barman, who gave her a chin lift and flirty wink in return and headed toward the VIP section. That was where she needed to be. That was where Carter would be, or where his minions would congregate in his absence.

It was too easy to get past the huge bouncer guarding the stairs to the VIP section. A smile and a pout as his eyes moved over her breasts and down her legs. "Nice ink, gorgeous."

Duchess gave him a coy look as she ran her hand over the tattoo on his bicep. "I could say the same, handsome."

He was like putty in her hands, and seconds later she could feel his eyes on her as she headed up the stairs. She turned and gave him a wink, and he smirked, thinking he was playing her.

Meathead men would never learn to stop under-estimating women, and it would be their downfall every single time.

The top floor was as she expected, and similar to Carter's other nightclubs in Leeds. A bar along the back, a balcony area with a dance floor that overlooked the main dance floor below, and comfortable black leather couches to the left of the bar area with low tables. Scattered around the right side were high tables with bar stools.

The waitresses were all stunning girls, of no more than twenty-five she'd guess, with short silver sequin dresses that left their backs naked and exposed to the lecherous looks and, most likely, touches of the men.

Duchess looked around the dance floor, which was mainly women, her gaze aiming toward the couches where a few known associates of Carter's sat around drinking. Two had girls in their laps, their hands wandering up their dresses.

Knocking back a little of the drink in her hand, she set it aside and headed that way. As she passed the bar, she saw a commotion at the top of the stairs. Carter and two of his men had arrived.

Excitement buzzed through her. This was perfect, she could hover on the periphery and see what she could make out. He was greeted like a king, hands shaken and a drink placed in his hand before he could ask. She watched him devour the waitress, his hands on her ass, lifting her dress as he kissed her neck and whispered something in her ear that made her giggle.

It disgusted her on every level, mostly because she could see past the veneer to the snake underneath. Andrea, Charlie's sister had been taken in by his charm in the same way. Getting pregnant by him and ending up locked away as part of 'Project Cradle' until they'd rescued her.

She wanted to get these girls away from him, to scream at them that he was poison dressed up as the dream they all craved, but she couldn't. The best she could do was take him down, and his criminal friends with him, and to do that she had to stop standing there like a voyeur at a sex club and head over and engage with them.

A hand wrapping tightly around her upper arm made her whirl automatically towards the threat. Duchess stopped the upward momentum of her fist just in time when she found herself pinned by the furious, electric blue eyes of Gideon Cavendish.

CHAPTER 4

"Wʜᴀᴛ ᴛʜᴇ ꜰᴜᴄᴋ ᴀʀᴇ ʏᴏᴜ ᴅᴏɪɴɢ ʜᴇʀᴇ?"

When he'd first seen her across the dance floor of the VIP section of Inferno, he'd had to take a second look. This woman wasn't the buttoned-up Miss Benassi he had to deal with at work. No, this woman was a fucking menace. She was fierce and more beautiful than any human had the right to be and seeing her exposed with all that stunning artwork on her warm, silken skin only enhanced his attraction to her. He'd thought earlier he'd been getting a handle on his wild attraction to the annoying woman but this raised it so many levels it was a wonder he hadn't dragged her to the nearest dark space so he could shove his dick inside her wet cunt.

"Get your fucking hands off me."

Duchess wrenched her arm from his grasp, and he let go, but kept himself in front of her body, shielding her from the wandering eyes of every man in the room. She had no idea how beautiful she was, or how thirsty she made every man who looked at her. "Why the hell are you here, Nadia?"

"Well, duh, why would I possibly be at your brother's club?"

She placed a finger over her red lips, and he felt his body respond.

He gritted his jaw and ground his teeth, trying to resist the urge to throw her over his shoulder and leave with her. "I told you I'd get you access."

"It's taking too long."

"What's the matter, Nadia, can't you handle working for me? The pressure too much for you at the top?"

He watched her roll her eyes and cross her arms over her chest, pushing her breasts higher in her dress. His eyes dipped to the warm skin and his fingers twitched to see if she was as soft as she looked, so he closed his hand into a fist to stop the reaction.

"I can handle whatever you dish out, Gideon. So don't worry your little brain about that."

"You're a bit of a bitch, you know that, right?"

"Better a bitch than a controlling asshole."

"I'm a controlling asshole? That's rich coming from you."

"Fuck you."

"You wish."

"Not even if our only job was to repopulate Earth after a fucking asteroid strike."

"Liar. I bet if I slipped my fingers between your legs right now, you'd be soaking wet for me." Gideon wondered if she could hear the desire in his voice.

He saw the pulse in her neck beating hard and knew he was right. His hand grasped her hip and pulled her close, her body seeming to move against her will, her hands falling to his chest.

"Are you, Duchess? Are you wet for me?"

"Fuck you."

She didn't deny it and she didn't move or try to get away, she was as mesmerised by him as he was by her. It was a relief to know it wasn't just him under this weird, fucked-up spell.

"You know I could find a much better use for that mouth than you cussing me."

His head dipped to her neck, his lips a whisper away from her skin and her scent invaded his nostrils, drugging him even further.

He wanted to suck the pulse he'd seen hammering there and mark her, claim her as his so every fucking man in this club knew who she belonged to.

"Never."

He smiled against her skin, his lips brushing her throat and she shuddered. "Oh, yeah, this is happening, Duchess."

"Gideon."

His back snapped straight at the sound of his brother's voice, and he closed his eyes to snap himself out of the lust fog so he could turn and deal with Carter. He kept his arm around Nadia's back, his hand resting on her hip. Carter wasn't getting his hooks into her. He didn't care if she could take out the British Army alone with one arm tied behind her back, he wasn't leaving her alone with Carter.

"Carter."

His younger brother was handsome, with the same dark hair as he and Damon had inherited from their father, but he had his mother's cool grey eyes and most definitely her calculation and manipulation tactics.

"I wasn't aware you were coming to Inferno tonight."

He was speaking to him, but his eyes kept moving over Nadia and Gideon wanted to rip his eyes out with a spoon for even looking at her like he was. "I wanted to show my girl Inferno."

He felt Nadia tense in his arms, just the slightest movement, but enough to let him know she wasn't happy about this new arrangement. Carter looked at Nadia again and then held out his hand.

"Nice to meet you...."

She took the hand and shook it. "Nadia."

"Nadia?" He frowned as if searching for a memory and then grinned. "Your new personal assistant that you stole from poor Damon? I commend you, Gideon. She's a real beauty."

Gideon tried to force a smile past his lips but the urge to punch his brother was strong as he referred to Nadia like she was a piece of prime rib, not a living breathing woman who had more integrity, passion, and morals in her little finger than he could ever hope to have.

"She's so much more than that."

Gideon could feel her eyes on him, and he couldn't look at her, not wanting to let his brother out of his sight for even a second.

Carter's rich laughter rang out over the club, the beat of the music below drowning out the words he muttered.

His body tensed and he had the desire to punch him right between his eyes. He was so sick of dealing with the mess his spoiled, over-indulged brother made. So sick of cleaning up after him and tired of watching his father become a shell because he'd let things get so far before he'd seen what the woman he'd married and the man his youngest son had become.

"I didn't catch that?"

"I said she must have one hell of a pussy to rein you in, brother. Perhaps when you're done I might indulge myself."

Gideon saw red, his vision tunnelling as he went to step up to Carter and teach his brother some fucking manners, but the small hand on his chest stopped him and he looked away from Carter finally to see Nadia looking at him with adoration before she turned to Carter.

"Why would I have a burger after having fillet steak?"

God, he wanted to kiss her, but then he saw the fury cross his brother's face and tensed. Carter didn't like being made to feel like a fool and could be petty and cruel if he thought someone had slighted him. At fourteen, he'd had one of the housekeeping staff fired because she hadn't indulged his attention. Carter smiled, it didn't reach his eyes and he knew Nadia had just made a powerful enemy, but he was letting it go for now.

"I like her, brother. You should bring her over to the house. Mother would find her delightful."

Gideon just lifted his chin and ignored the invitation. Seeing Nadia and the wicked stepmother go toe to toe might be fun if the stepmother wasn't likely to poison the food and have the woodsman take her in the back and kill her.

"It's early days. Let's see how it goes before we have a family get together, hey?"

He saw suspicion on his brother's face and needed to get rid of any doubt. He was a leery bastard, thinking everyone was out to get him, and he'd be right on this occasion, but Gideon didn't want him to know that. Leaning close to Carter's ear, he spoke words that felt like a betrayal to Nadia. "Not sure the pussy is that good, brother."

Carter laughed and he did too, all the while hating his brother more and more.

"I'll leave you to it. Gideon, don't forget that file on Macey's I asked for. I have a contact that might be able to get us some inside information." His gaze slid to Nadia again and he licked his lips. "Perhaps have Nadia reach out to my secretary and arrange a time we can meet and discuss it."

"I will." He'd do nothing of the sort.

As Carter walked away, he kept his eyes on him, not trusting that snake in the grass in the slightest. As Carter was swallowed up by the throngs of women, clawing for his attention, he relaxed and looked down at Nadia.

She was still nestled under his arm, her body warm and soft against his much harder one and he liked it. He didn't want to. He wasn't a clingy cuddler and they weren't a couple or even fucking. Mostly they hated each other but he'd opened a door with her, by having Carter believe they were sleeping together and perhaps going down this route would be more fun than fighting with her. Maybe, just maybe, they could get this desire he felt and he knew she felt out of their system in a safe way without any feelings getting hurt.

"Well, I see being a dick runs in the family."

His chuckle made her pull back so she could see his face clearly, but he kept his arms around her waist, loving the feel of her there. "Tell me, Nadia, do you ever turn off this snippy side of your personality?"

Her lips twitched as if she wanted to smile but she fought it and won.

"No."

"Hmm, perhaps it's a good thing. Your fiery side makes my dick hard."

He took her hand and placed it over the bulge in his trousers. He knew he was pushing his luck, and the likelihood of a slap across the face was becoming more possible with every second, but when she touched him, he couldn't stop the groan or the flex of his hips, especially when she tightened her palm on his cock and squeezed. As if all the air was drawn from the room, she stepped closer, her hand still closed around his aching cock and he couldn't look away. Her lips moved over Gideon's cheek in the lightest caress before she let go and moved away.

"Goodnight, Gideon."

He watched her walk away, his eyes on her until he could no longer see her and then swung his gaze across the room to see his brother watching him carefully. Shrugging, he gave him a 'what can you do' look and made as if to follow her.

He didn't though, instead calling his driver, Saul, to pick him up.

In the back of the limo, which was how he always travelled, he poured himself a whiskey from the small bar in the back and knocked it back, savouring the burn in his throat. Tonight hadn't gone as he'd planned, and he hated that. Proper planning prevented piss poor performance, everyone knew that, and it was one of the earliest lessons his father had taught him.

Yet Nadia turning up had disrupted everything. Seeing her in the club, her body on display, not in a slutty way but in a way that drove men fucking crazy, was bad enough. But then really seeing her for the first time with her tattoos uncovered, fuck, he'd had no idea she was inked like that. She clearly covered up at work, whether that was as a way of keeping that part of herself private from the job she was really doing or because she knew it would make her that much more recognisable, he didn't know. He suspected it was a bit of both.

The car drew to a stop outside his building, and he got out. "See you in the morning, Saul."

"Goodnight, Mr Cavendish."

He took the stairs, needing to burn off some of the energy tingling beneath his skin. Reaching the door to his penthouse, he let himself in and headed straight for the bar. Another two inches of whiskey didn't help so he took the bottle and headed for the balcony.

Sinking down on the couch he had there, he let the beauty of the night settle over his skin. The bright lights of London twinkled; the hum of traffic way down below mingled with the other sounds of the night. The murmur of voices and life told of a city that never seemed to settle.

He loved it here, the vibrancy, the feeling of being in the middle of life somehow. It was the place he came to clear his mind but tonight it was full of her. What was it about her that made him so unstable, made him act so out of character?

His mind flitted over the memory of seeing her tattoos. He had them, one on his chest, the other on his right shoulder and bicep, but she had more, and they were stunning. Not detracting from her beauty but adding another layer to it and she was brave with them. Not scared to have them where they were most visible. Her arms, her neck, and shoulder and one that had teased him with a glimpse on her thigh.

It went against his earlier theory of why she covered them. A private person wouldn't have ink in places that made people ask questions, at least not a woman. He knew she was confident, a ball buster, and the thought made him smile again as he now sipped the whiskey.

Nadia was more complex than he'd first thought. He'd underestimated her, seeing what she allowed him to see. He realised now that there was more to her and fuck if it didn't make him want to strip all those layers back until he exposed the soft side of herself she kept for those she trusted with it.

Yet he knew, if he got to her soft underbelly, where she was vulnerable, he'd be incapable of doing anything with it. He wasn't made for commitment, he was too busy, too demanding, and he didn't believe in letting anyone see his weaknesses. So why was he suddenly so desperate to expose hers for himself?

Was it because he saw her as a worthy adversary or was it because she held the key to eradicating this weight from his shoulders and freeing him and Damon from the shadow of Carter and Marsha?

As the sky began to turn from the dark pitch of night to the navy of coming daylight, he still had no answers. Standing, he felt exhaustion move over him. Not just from his night of deep thinking but from years of not sleeping properly and holding the company up on his shoulders.

It would be nice to have a partner in this, someone who could ease the burden and share the weight but that involved trust and he couldn't take that risk again. He'd trusted his mother not to leave him and she had.

As he shucked his clothes and crawled into his huge bed and lay looking at the ceiling, he thought of his mother and her sweetness, but also her strength. She'd fought cancer and lost but she'd fought and fought until one day there was no fight left and she'd been gone in the blink of an eye. He'd never let someone have that kind of power over him again.

As he closed his eyes, it wasn't his mother's face he saw though, it was Nadia's when she looked at him when he'd defended her to Carter as if she was really seeing him for the first time.

It made him feel warm, his chest heavy and tingly and he liked it. So much so he knew he'd need to shut that down and quick. Whatever they had or didn't have, the priority was taking down Carter. Not this wild attraction to the girl with rose tattoos.

CHAPTER 5

Monday morning wasn't going as she expected. Her head hung over the toilet bowl as she exhausted the contents of her empty stomach until it felt like her insides were falling out, wasn't her idea of fun.

She'd woken in the middle of the night feeling achy and hot after a day spent watching surveillance footage of Carter from Saturday night in the club. Watchdog had already reviewed it, but she wanted to go over it herself and see if she picked up any nuances that perhaps someone not so close to the case might not.

She'd made it to the bathroom just in time as her stomach revolted, and she'd thrown up. After the third trip from her bed, she'd given up and curled into a ball on the bathroom floor and rested there.

Nadia never got sick, she always seemed to avoid bugs, but this fucker had got her good. Her lids heavy, she let them fall shut as she considered how she'd get herself up and dressed for work.

Her phone ringing woke her with a start and, as she moved too quickly, her entire body shivered, her stomach cramping. Trying to decide if she should run for the phone or puke, the decision was taken out of her hands as she sagged back against the toilet. She must have fallen asleep with her head on her arms, resting on the toilet lid, because she was woken again by a banging on her front door.

"Duchess, open up."

Hurricane.

Sitting up slowly this time, she managed to get to her feet and crawl as far as the couch.

"Duchess, are you okay?"

"I'm sick," she called out. "I have the stomach flu."

Silence greeted her and she almost smiled.

"Oh, uh. You need anything?"

It was widely known Hurricane wasn't great with sick people and was the worst when he himself got sick.

"No, unless you want to shoot me and put me out of my misery."

"Uh, yeah, no. I'm gonna go let Bás know you're alive."

"Fine, tell him I'll call him tomorrow."

"Yeah, will do."

She heard him walk away and curled up on her couch, her body shivering until her teeth rattled. The clock on the wall said it was ten am and she knew Gideon would be furious he'd had to get his own coffee and most likely call in a temp. She should call in really, but she didn't have the strength to get up from her couch and get her phone from her nightstand.

Thirty minutes later she was dozing, thinking how death would be preferable to this hell when there was a thunderous knock on her door.

"For fuck's sake, can't a girl die in peace without the entire world banging on her door?"

Rousing the tiny bit of energy she had, she stumbled to the door and yanked it open ready to tell Hurricane to get lost, but it wasn't her friend, it was Gideon. "Gideon?"

He looked gorgeous in a navy blue tailored suit with a white shirt and silver-grey tie. His hair was slightly mussed, but his electric blue eyes took her in and she knew she looked like hell.

"You look like the living dead."

She didn't have the energy to fight him today. "Urgh, just go, let me die in peace." She moved to shut the door on his pretty face but was hit by a wave of dizziness that had the floor pitching toward her.

"Woah." Strong arms caught her descent and then she was weightless, burrowed into a warm, hard chest as she shivered from head to toe. He sat with her in his lap on her old couch and held her tight. He was so warm she wanted to crawl inside him until her teeth stopped chattering.

A hand touched her forehead and then her neck. "Jesus, you're burning up."

"I'm gross, you need to go."

His chuckle rumbled beneath her. "You are gross, but I'm not leaving you like this."

He stood and hesitated a second before carrying her to her bedroom. Gideon was in her space, taking over, commanding, and she didn't have it in her to fight him. He laid her down on the cool sheets in her bed and covered her with the quilt, tucking it to her chin.

"We need to cool you down. This should be stripped off you really."

"If you take this quilt away, I'll remove your lungs with a spoon while you sleep."

Another chuckle sounded as gentle fingers swept her hair back from her sweaty neck.

"Not sure you could fight your way out of a wet paper bag right now, Cookie."

She felt him stand and walk away and wondered if he was leaving. Part of her felt relief but the other part was sad he was leaving her. It was an indication of how sick she must be if she wanted him to take care of her. Being ill always made her emotional for her dad. He'd been the caretaker in the family, bringing her soup and sitting with her on the couch to watch trashy movies.

Gideon was back a few minutes later, his jacket missing, and his sleeves rolled up his tan, muscular forearms. He placed a glass of water on the bedside table and put his hand under her neck to lift her head.

"Here, take these. It will help reduce your fever."

A giant shudder wracked her body as he held the glass to her lips, her teeth rattling the glass.

"Open."

Duchess opened her mouth and he placed two tablets on her tongue. She idly wondered how disgusting she must smell with her sweaty body and vomit breath, but she had no energy to really care.

Gideon disappeared again, returning with a wet flannel that he placed against her brow.

"No, it's cold." She began to fight him. He grasped her wrist tightly but not so tight it hurt.

"Don't be a baby. We need to get your fever down. So, unless you want me to strip you down and plunk you in a cold bath, take the flannel."

Duchess relented because the alternative sounded like torture.

Soft, heavy hands stroked her hair and back as he read on his phone. "It says here most bugs like this only last a few days at most. How long have you been sick?"

"Middle of the night."

Her body was growing heavy again and the sound of his voice was soothing her into sleep. The deep baritone was reassuring and comforting. His touch made her feel less alone in this bacterium-induced hell.

She woke sometime later, no longer shivering but aching in every part of her body. As she turned to sit up, nausea hit her hard and she threw back the covers and staggered to the bathroom. Falling to her knees, she wretched, her empty stomach contracting painfully.

The feel of hands grasping her long hair from her face and holding it, while rubbing her back, made her tense as she tried to find the threads of memory just out of reach. Collapsing onto the floor, she looked up as strong arms lifted her.

"You done for now?"

Gideon! Oh God, this was worse than she thought.

"Put me down."

"No."

He walked to her bedroom and eased her into the bed, covering her again as she tried to convince herself this was a nightmare and this hot, annoying, asshole wasn't in her flat looking after her while she puked her guts out.

"Here, drink, but small sips. You're most likely dehydrated from being so sick."

His hand curled around hers on the glass to steady her and she drank, hoping it didn't cause her stomach to revolt again.

Sinking back against the pillows, she eyed him and saw he'd taken off his tie and undone the top two buttons of his shirt, revealing smooth, tan skin.

"Why are you here?"

"You're sick."

"I know that, but why did you come here and why are you still here? You don't even like me."

She saw his brow crease as he sat on the edge of her bed. "Why would you think that?"

Duchess felt her eyes bug from her head. "Um, the fact you're an absolute dick most of the time."

He chuckled and it made his Adam's apple bob, drawing her eyes to his throat before she glanced up into his face. Why did he have to be so fucking hot?

"Do you always say what's on your mind?"

"No, it's these drugs you made me take."

"They're hardly drugs, Nadia. They're just pain relief, not some kind of truth serum."

"Whatever." She turned on her side so he couldn't see her face as she snuggled under the covers, tiredness invading her body as the aches seemed to recede a little.

"I do like you, Nadia." He paused and she wondered if he had more to say. "You just get under my skin, and nobody gets under my skin."

"Because you're Mr Controlling."

"Maybe, but I have my reasons."

"Damon is nothing like you."

His jaw clenched, his eyes going flinty. "Well, Damon is the best of us."

"He's my friend."

"I know."

"I wish I could want Damon, he's a good guy."

"You don't want a good guy, Nadia. You'd chew him up and spit him out within a week."

"How do you know what I want?"

"Because we're the same. We both want to be in control. It's why I need to keep my distance from you when all I want to do is sink inside you and make you scream my name."

Duchess felt her heart thud in her chest, her pulse skittering around like Tigger on speed.

"Oh."

"Oh? That's all it took to make you speechless. If I'd known that I would've told you weeks ago."

"What do you want me to say?"

"I don't know, nothing, everything." He ran his fingers through his hair. "Just forget it and get some rest. I'm going to go do some work in that tiny space you call a living area."

"You don't have to stay. I'll be fine on my own."

A growl seemed to slip past his lips as he stood. "I'm not fucking leaving you to fend for yourself while you're sick. Just get some sleep, I'll be back with your medication later."

She watched him move to the door. "Gideon?"

He turned back, the annoyed expression he usually wore firmly in place.

"Thank you."

His eyes creased as his jaw softened. "No problem, Cookie."

When he was like this it was so much harder to hate him, to fight the attraction that was so strong it almost made her forget all her own rules. Gideon, she was realising, wasn't just the arrogant asshole he showed the world. He was so much more than that, and it was deadly to her resolve to stay away from him.

CHAPTER 6

GIDEON LOOKED UP FROM THE REPORT HE WAS READING AS HIS DOOR OPENED and was stupidly pleased to see Nadia standing in his doorway. She was looking much better than the last time he'd seen her, her hair shining, her skin a healthier shade, and her eyes were no longer bright with fever.

He let his eyes move over the tattoos she was no longer covering, admiring the artwork on her skin. In his opinion this would be too much on most women, giving them a hardness he didn't like, but on her, it worked.

She wore her usual office attire of a blouse and pencil skirt, this time a pale pink blouse and black skirt. Her hair was up in a ponytail, away from the neck he'd thought about kissing too many times.

"Good morning, Mr Cavendish."

"Good morning, Miss Benassi. How are you feeling?"

A blush stained her cheeks, surprising and delighting him.

"Much better, thank you. I had a very unexpected but excellent nurse looking after me."

Now it was his turn to blush. "Are those my papers?" Gideon held out his hand for his morning papers, which he still liked to read for the financial section.

"Yes, and here's your coffee from that place you like with the organic beans."

His eyebrows rose in surprise. "Thank you, but what's the occasion?"

He sniffed the coffee and sipped cautiously as she laughed.

"It's not poisoned. I just wanted to say thank you for, you know, taking care of me."

"Well, it was an experience that's for sure, but I had to make sure we got you back in the office quick smart. I haven't got time to train another PA."

"Well, either way, thank you."

He pursed his lips and dipped his head, not finding it easy to receive thanks from anyone.

He watched her walk from the room and turned to his emails. He had an invitation to a ball a week from Friday and he knew Damon and Carter would be attending and, most likely, the step-demon from hell. It would be the perfect opportunity for Nadia to meet them both and see if she could glean anything new. He closed the email without responding. He should take her, but he had the overwhelming urge to protect her.

Since finding her almost passed out from illness, he'd seen a side to Nadia he was fairly sure she didn't show to many people. A gentler, vulnerable side and, for the first time since his mother had died, he'd felt the urge to care for someone and nurture them.

Sure, he still wanted to fuck her brains out but something more was stirring beneath the surface, and he couldn't place it. Now, the thought of her putting herself on the line or in the way of danger made him want to stand between her and any perils she might face.

A few hours later a knock on his door had him looking up. "Come."

As the door opened, he went to stand as his father walked into the room. "Dad, what are you doing here?"

Gideon nodded at Nadia that it was okay and she closed the door, leaving them alone.

"Can't a man visit his son at work without the third degree?"

"Of course, but you don't."

His father sighed and Gideon noticed how he was really looking his age, the twinkle in his eye was dimmed, he had black circles around his eyes, and he'd lost weight. It reminded him too much of how his mother had looked when she was sick.

"The new girl is different. I thought I was going to have to fight her to get to you."

"Miss Benassi is very good at her job and protects my time as instructed."

"There was a time when everyone in this company knew who I was and respected my position."

Nadia knew exactly who his father was, she wasn't just a PA, although she was excellent at it.

"You stopped coming around and the staff rotate and move on."

"Hmm, seems so."

His father wandered around the office until he was standing in front of the window looking out over London. This had been his office once, his domain and seat of power but he'd handed it over and, as far as Gideon was concerned, he'd lost the right when he fucked it up so royally that they'd almost gone under. It had taken blood, sweat and tears from Gideon to save this company and turn it around, especially with a boot on his neck in the form of Carter and Marsha.

"Why are you here, Dad?"

His father put his hands in the pockets of his trousers and turned to him. "I need you to let Carter help with the Macey deal."

Everything in Gideon revolted against the request. "No."

"Son, please. Just let him be involved and help out."

"No fucking way. You know the shit he's involved with. Why do you insist on trying to drag this company, which you and mum built, into the gutter?"

"Don't be dramatic. Carter is just more of a risk-taker than you. Perhaps you could learn something from him."

Gideon closed his eyes, breathing through his nose to try and get a rein on his temper which was about to explode. "Are you fucking kidding me? I sweat blood getting this company back on its feet and not once did you thank me. Not once did you apologise for the shit you pulled. Damon was the only support I had as we turned this around and made it the highly successful enterprise it is, and now you want me to let Carter get his dirty paws on a deal that could take us to the next level?"

"Yes, you need to do this. I still have sway with the board, Gideon. Don't make me use it."

Gideon shook his head, his gut twisting in anger and betrayal. "Wow, after everything you know he's involved with, you still choose him over me."

"Grow up, Gideon this isn't playschool. This is business."

"Yes, a business that you wouldn't have if it wasn't for me."

"I could say the same. I built this company."

"No, you and mum built this company and now you're going to let that piece of trash and her spawn ruin it."

"Watch your mouth, Gideon."

"Fuck that. You can speak to the board, sack me, whatever you need to do, but make no mistake, Carter isn't getting near this deal. He is a criminal. He's nothing but venom leaking into everything he touches and if you want to take his side, then have at it."

"Son, I don't want to threaten you, but you leave me no choice. I'm…" His father stopped and looked back to the window before speaking again. "I'm in trouble and I have fewer choices than you do."

Gideon regarded his dad with caution, the trust between them long broken with lies and hidden truths. "What kind of trouble?"

"The kind that will end up with me in a box or at the bottom of a river."

"What the hell? Talk to me, Dad."

"I,...I can't but I need your help. You don't have to do anything else but let Carter take a seat at the table on this deal."

"And if I do this, you'll be safe?"

His father let out a shaky breath and Gideon wished he didn't care.

"Yes."

"Let me think about it."

"I can give you until tomorrow morning, son."

"Fine."

The silence that shrouded the room was heavy and oppressive, and he felt like he was choking on it. A knock seemed to relieve the pressure and let him drag in some much-needed air. "Yes?"

Seeing Nadia was like a balm. He could feel the tension in his chest ease as she smiled at him.

"I'm sorry to disturb you, Mr Cavendish, but you have that urgent meeting you asked me to set up."

He'd done no such thing, but she seemed to know he needed a lifeline and had thrown it before he drowned. "Yes, thank you."

He held out his hand to his father and walked him to the door. "I'll call you tomorrow morning with my answer."

His father looked between him and Nadia and smiled, giving him a wink. "Of course, son."

As he walked away, Gideon fought to remember the good things from his childhood, the man who'd taught him to swim and ride a bike because the one leaving this office wasn't him.

Turning, he saw Nadia watching him and knew he needed help. He needed advice and she was the only person he could talk to or felt comfortable talking to about this. "I need to speak with you in my office, Miss Benassi."

"Of course, sir. Would you like me to order lunch first?"

The way she said sir made his dick harden instantly. The thought of her in that tight skirt on her knees calling him sir sent white hot lust coursing through his body.

"No, change of plans. Let's go out for lunch, we can talk in the car."

Surprise flickered over her face briefly. "Okay, would you like me to book somewhere?"

"No, the place I have in mind doesn't need a booking."

"I'll just get my bag then."

Gideon waited while she grabbed her bag from the bottom drawer of her desk and then looked up at him.

He led her toward the elevator, his hand on the small of her back feeling natural, his urge to touch her in some small way wasn't something he wanted to examine right now. Nor how the feelings of rejection and anger his father had evoked seemed to dissipate when she was around.

As Saul opened the car door for her, he watched her glance around discreetly as if looking for someone. He followed her gaze but saw nothing out of the ordinary and wondered if it wasn't just an ingrained habit for her to be cautious.

As she settled back against the leather seat, pushing her skirt over her knees, he sensed the questions she was holding in and was grateful for the time to wrangle his thoughts into some kind of order.

As they neared his penthouse, he glanced sideways and knew she was aware of where he lived. She probably knew every secret he had and yet he felt like he hardly knew this woman who was tying him up in knots.

The light from the sunny late autumn day was hazy and low in the sky as they pulled up outside his building. There was a tranquil almost expectant feel to the air as if summer was having a last hurrah before the cold and rain of winter hit with force.

He kept his briefcase between him and Nadia so as to resist the need to touch her again. Nadia, seeming to sense his need for quiet, had held any questions she had about his father's visit to herself.

As they had sped towards his penthouse, he had wondered what she'd think about his home. Would she find it cold and uninviting?

Would she see the touches of himself in the design that he'd helped the designer create, and more importantly, why did he care?

As they stepped into the foyer, he watched her take in the high ceilings before moving to the mezzanine level and then the wrap-around terrace that had views of the London Eye in the distance.

"Wow, this wasn't what I expected at all."

Gideon cocked his head and threw his briefcase on the sofa and headed to the kitchen. "No? What did you expect?"

He saw her run her hands over the fabric of his couch as she wandered through the open concept space toward him where he stood at the island watching her.

"Well, obviously I knew where you lived, but I don't know. I guess I imagined it would be whiter, more clinical."

Gideon chuckled. "Well, the designer wanted white, but I wanted a home, not an operating theatre. But still the clean lines and minimalism."

"I like it, it suits you."

"Thank you."

Reaching into her bag, he saw her retrieve a small device and switch it on. "What is that?"

Nadia held up a finger to her lips.

"Nothing, just my lip palette."

As he watched, she ran the device over his furniture, moving from room to room as he followed like a lost child. As he moved closer, he could guess what it was and why she was checking, but it had never occurred to him to check his home for bugs.

As she pushed open the door of his bedroom, she glanced at the bed and he had the deepest desire to see her sprawled out there, her hair spread out across the pillow, lips swollen from his kisses.

"You have a wonderful view of London. Do you use the terrace a lot?"

He frowned, confused by the small talk until she pointed at the flashing light, and he saw it blinking, and his eyes widened.

Son of a bitch. "I do. I love being out there, especially at night, it helps me relax."

"I bet. I'd live out here if this place were mine."

As she reached his bedside clock and flipped it upside down, she pointed to the small bug that looked like a microchip, and he balled his fists in anger.

As they moved through his home, they found another in his home office, one in the gym, and another under the light of his outdoor lighting panel.

As they passed the bathroom, she pulled him inside by his sleeve and switched on the tap.

"What do you want to do, leave them in place or get rid of them?"

Gideon was a little shocked by the turn of events and his gut reaction was that he wanted them gone. He felt violated by the thought of someone listening in on him in his home. How long had they been there and who had planted them?

"I don't know. What should I do?"

Nadia pursed her lips and he saw a different side to her than the woman who ran his life at work like damn clockwork.

"Well, if you leave them you have to know someone is listening at all times or at least recording and monitoring, but they won't realise we're onto them. If we get rid of them, you'll rest easier knowing you can speak freely in your home, but they'll know we found them and are potentially on to them."

"What would you do?"

"It's different for me, Gideon. I live a very different life to you. I'm always guarded about what I say and to whom. If you're asking me what you should do, I'd destroy them. They clearly suspect you know something, or they wouldn't be monitoring your home and the chances of slipping up are high."

"Okay, let's do that." He was surprised by his own capitulation. He was letting her lead and that was unusual for him.

Nadia nodded and went to turn the tap off, but he caught her arm. "What about the office?"

"I check that every morning and evening, so far it's been clear."

Gideon nodded, his gut churning with the realisation that this was getting very real now, or perhaps it was always real and he was just late in figuring it out.

He once again followed Nadia around and she dealt with the bugs, popping one in her purse so she could have her people look at it and see if they could source it.

"My bag is lined so it won't work inside there."

"I see."

"I need to call Bás and the team in on this."

"Fine, but I need to talk to you about my father's visit."

CHAPTER 7

Nadia watched Gideon's face twist as he said the words. He'd been unusually placid the last hour and she knew some of it was the shock of finding bugs in his home, but it had started before that.

"I thought you might."

He held his palm out, gesturing her towards the sofa and she sat, angling her body towards him as he took the seat beside her, his arm thrown over the back of the couch. It was supposed to reflect an open, honest posture, but she could practically feel the tension radiating off him. "Talk to me."

His jaw flexed with strain, so she reached out, placing a hand over his arm on the back of the couch. His eyes slid to hers and she saw the heat turn his bright blue eyes slumberous. She wasn't the kind of woman to wax poetic about a man, but Gideon seemed to drag her in as if he wanted to drown her in the feelings he evoked in her body.

Desire pooled in her belly, her thighs clenching to ease the ache his look caused her. The air was electrified with lust and sex. It was as if that one innocent touch had lit a fuse and there was no taking it back. Each of them was paralysed by it until they were both moving at once.

His hands were threaded through her hair, loosening the ponytail she'd worn that morning. His lips crashed against hers, soft and firm as he slid his tongue against the seam of her mouth. She opened it with a sigh as he dragged her across his lap. The hardness she felt beneath her core as she straddled him made her ache to feel him inside her.

His hands skimmed her rib cage, moving over the side of her breast, causing her nipples to peak as he grasped her throat in his hand. His thumb circled over the pulse on the side of her neck as he cocked his head to watch her. "You're so fucking beautiful, Cookie."

Her hands moved under his jacket, hating the fabric that separated them from warm skin. She knew his body was fit but as she touched him, feeling the ridges of stacked muscle underneath her fingertips, she wanted to see more, to see all of him.

His hard cock rocked against her clit and she moaned as he swallowed it down with his mouth on hers, a growl vibrating in his chest. "Fuck, I can feel how wet you are through my trousers."

A whimper tore from her as he thrust up, pushing her body toward the climax she was so desperate to feel. Gideon let his free hand move down her body as he pinched her nipple through the flimsy material of her blouse. Her hips arched against him, seeking the friction of his cock.

"Take it, Nadia. Take your pleasure from me. Let me watch as you come all over me."

"Gideon?"

Duchess froze at the sound of Damon's voice, ringing through the apartment. Scrambling off his lap, she glanced at Gideon who was standing to button his jacket. Duchess put more space between them, turning to the pictures above the fireplace as she gave herself a moment to reset her equilibrium and get a handle on her emotions and her body. She had been so damn close to climax and her body felt like a bow drawn tight and not allowed to fly.

What the hell had she been thinking dry humping Gideon in his living room, just after finding his home riddled with bugs? Shame and anger with herself washed over her as she heard the voice in the foyer move closer.

Pasting a bright smile on her face, she prayed her lip stain was still in place as she turned to see Damon stop at the entrance to the living area.

"Duchess, what are you doing here?"

"I needed to speak to her in private about Dad."

Damon frowned as he focused his attention on Gideon. "Dad?"

Gideon walked to the bar and poured himself a drink, lifting the crystal decanter to his brother and her as they both shook their heads, no.

"Yes, father dearest came to visit me at the office."

"Oh?"

Damon sat on the couch and Duchess tried not to let the blush stain her skin as she thought of what had been going on there only moments ago. Gideon caught her eye and smirked and she wanted to wipe the smug grin off his face.

"Yes, your father came in to see Gideon."

Damon looked between them as if sensing the tension and narrowed his eyes. Duchess could feel the censure in the look and hated that she was disappointing her friend. And that was what he'd become over the last year of working with him before she ended up as Gideon's PA.

"What did he want?"

"Oh, you know the usual, for me to let Carter help with the Macey deal."

Damon stood, his face outraged as he went to the bar and poured himself a drink, clearly thinking he needed it now. "Help how?" Nadia asked.

Gideon locked eyes with her at her question. "He wants him involved in the negotiations and to have access to everything."

"We can't let him have access to that deal. I hope you told him no."

"Jeez, Damon, why didn't I think of that?"

Gideon rolled his eyes and Duchess studied the by-play between the brothers. They weren't buddy-buddy close but seeing their dynamic made her think they had been once, and perhaps still were in some ways. They just weren't effusive with it.

"Well, what did you say?"

"I said no fucking way."

Gideon ran a hand through his hair, and she could see the stress he was feeling in the slope of his shoulders, and how much the visit had affected him.

"He threatened you again, didn't he?"

Her eyes swung to Damon. "What?"

He wasn't looking at her though, he was spearing his brother with a worried gaze.

"Yes."

"What did you say?"

"I told him to do his worst, but he'll follow through this time, I could see in his eyes."

Duchess moved closer, placing herself between them as she held her hand up to Damon and looked at Gideon. "What did he threaten you with?" It didn't sit right with her that while she'd been outside the door, Gideon had been threatened.

Gideon sighed and sat heavily on the couch. "He said he'd go to the board and force a vote of no confidence in me and have me stripped of my title and therefore any power."

"Can he do that?"

"Yes."

"Why is your father such a dick to you two?"

Damon sat down beside his older brother in a show of support who, at that second, looked defeated and exhausted. "He isn't pulling his own strings anymore. He hasn't been since he met Marsha."

"Even so."

Gideon looked up at her. "That's not all. He says he owes money to some bad people, and they're going to kill him unless he can pull this off." He glanced at Damon. "He was scared."

"Fuck him. He's never given us anything but headaches, not since the day they laid Mum in the ground."

"If we say yes, this deal with Macey's will sink us. Carter will see to it. He has an agenda here. He has enough money from his illegal shit to keep him happy, so money isn't it."

Gideon got up and paced, grasping the back of his neck as he did, looking more dishevelled by the second, and yet still sexy as hell. "I can start again. I have an offer from Chelsea Bank to go and work for them."

"No." Damon slashed his hand through the air as if to finalise his thoughts. "No. You worked yourself to the bone to save this company after he almost bankrupted us and I won't see you forced out because of that little prick."

"What other choice do we have? If I say no, he forces me out. If I say yes, we lose anyway."

"Not necessarily." Both men turned to her when she spoke, and it was striking to see the differences and yet the similarities between them side by side.

"If you have a plan, then now is a good time to voice it," Gideon demanded, but with slightly less asshole than his usual flavour.

"The bugs in your apartment prove they suspect you. I think they're banking on you saying no and being forced out. That way someone else, likely Carter, will step in and have free rein to do as he pleases."

"Wait, what?" Damon jumped to his feet as he watched her.

"We found bugs all over this place. Not sure how long they've been there but someone with access planted them."

"Jesus Christ."

"Yes, exactly. I propose we say yes, but you counter and tell your Dad you'll only agree if Carter cuts you into the deal. Tell him you know he has a contact at Macey's and you want in on it. He'll believe you're coming around, especially as you've been running the underground casinos for him."

Gideon blanched. "Excuse me? I've been doing no such thing."

Duchess rolled her lips. "According to every paper trail we have, you are, and there's footage of you going in and out too."

"Bullshit."

His venom proved Hurricane's theory right. He was being used as the fall guy just as he had with the trail of men leading back to Gideon that had attacked the house resulting in Charlie getting shot.

"We have pictures and files with your signature on them."

She needed to push just to make sure, but her gut was telling her she was right, and so was Hurricane.

"I don't give a fuck if you have a confession signed in my blood, they're wrong."

Gideon looked angry, and a little rattled and she realised she didn't like seeing him that way. Making a decision, she decided to give Gideon and Damon her trust and hoped it didn't come back to bite her in the ass. Bás wouldn't like it, but her intuition and ability to adapt on the fly was one of the reasons they worked well together. "What do you know of Project Cradle?"

Gideon wrinkled his nose in confusion. "Project what?"

Duchess sat on the coffee table and faced the brothers, ignoring her attraction to Gideon and the residual lust coursing through her veins. "Project Cradle was set up by the CIA in the nineties. It took volunteers of pregnant women who felt that they had no other choices. The CIA took the babies and trained and educated them from birth to be fighters and assets for the CIA. But they only took female babies and, after a while, it stopped being voluntary."

"Jesus Christ."

Damon looked shocked and it made her pause that she didn't find it shocking. This was her world, the one she inhabited anyway.

"I know, it's bad."

"It was later shut down but before that, the then director of the

CIA, a man named Mills, signed his daughter up. The story is she'd got in with a bad lot and got pregnant and although the details are sketchy, we think her father didn't approve of the baby's father. Her name was Molly Mills but after her falling out with her father, she changed her name."

Duchess paused, wondering how this would go down, but knowing they needed to know the truth. Gideon met her eyes and she saw he knew whatever she said next would change everything.

"What did she change it to?"

"Marsha Morales."

Gideon sat forward as if someone had punched him in the gut, and winded him. "Holy fucking hell."

"We don't know if she had the child, and if she did what happened to it. But we do know she was involved with Project Cradle after it was allegedly shut down."

"You mean it wasn't shut down?"

"Officially, yes. But a few rogue agents got together with some private businessmen and a new Project Cradle was born. Now it's privately funded, and the children are hand-picked from either already pregnant women, where the father is known and approved, or from young girls that the members have impregnated."

"You think our father is involved?"

"Not directly but we know Carter is up to his eyeballs in it. He's one of the major players and moneymen. He's also involved in getting the girls pregnant. We recently rescued a group of women from one of his properties and one was carrying his child. She was the sister of one of our operators."

Damon slapped a hand over his mouth. "I'm gonna be sick."

He rushed from the room and Duchess looked at him with sympathy. It was a lot for anyone to take in and Damon had a soft heart.

Her gaze drifted to Gideon who looked pale and shaken. "Are you okay?"

His haunted eyes lifted to her face. "I don't know."

"I'm sorry."

He cocked his head. "What for? You didn't do any of this."

"Still, I'm sorry you're having to learn all of this."

"Yeah? Well, I'm sorry I've been such an asshole when you're just trying to fix such a mess."

Duchess smirked. "Well, seeing as you did hold my hair while I puked my guts out, I'll forgive you."

His grin made her belly tumble over and she wished she could go to him and make him feel better. But as much as she wanted to, it wasn't her job to make him feel better.

Damon returned with a glass of water and sat. "Sorry about that."

"It's fine."

"What happened to the girl? Was she okay?"

"She will be, but she lost the baby."

Gideon looked down at his hands. "Fuck."

"And the others? You said there were more."

"Yes, they've been moved to a secure facility where they'll get the help they need."

Gideon nodded. "Good, good."

"You say the girls are picked or chosen and some are impregnated by members, and others picked when they're already pregnant?" Damon asked.

"Yes. Carter has a string of fertility and obstetrics clinics around the country and some in other countries and, while they do operate a legitimate side, when they have a girl come in who fits the profile, young, alone, with no support, they'll check the background and run the DNA and then decide if she'll be used."

"Fertility clinics?"

Gideon was recovering from his shock now.

"Yes, they're legitimate holdings."

"How come we don't know about them?"

"It wasn't done under his name. It's a shell company, so there's no reason why you would as it isn't tied to Cavendish in any way."

"And by used, you mean kidnapped, and her baby stolen from her?"

"Yes."

Damon sipped the water. "What happens afterwards?"

"We think the mothers are either kept as breeding stock, killed, or the younger ones are sex trafficked."

"How has nobody figured this out already?"

"Because there are some very powerful people involved and they're clever and connected."

"You said some were already pregnant but there are ones who are impregnated by the members?" Gideon swallowed and she could tell from his ashen face how hard he was finding this, so she softened her tone.

"Yes, from what we know some are runaways, others are tricked into prostitution at the clubs and then sperm is used from one of the high-ranking members in some kind of awful insemination process. Others, the ones…" She paused because even she found this hard, and she'd had years of dealing with the worst of humanity.

Gideon reached out and threaded his fingers through hers and she sucked in a shaky breath, seeing her paler skin against his tan hand, their fingers woven together. She ignored the questioning look Damon was giving them because there was nothing sexual about the touch, at least not overtly. There was strength in his touch, but it was meant for comfort, a sign to her that he was in this with her and despite having her team who she adored this felt different. Right in a way she didn't want to explain even to herself.

"The ones the members find attractive are either seduced into a relationship with the men or taken without consent."

Gideon dropped his head and squeezed her hand before letting go. "Jesus Christ. I knew Carter was a piece of shit but to find him involved with this is sickening on a level I can hardly process."

"How do you know all this, Duchess?"

She turned to see Damon share a look with Gideon, an unspoken conversation between siblings. Damon looked as heartsick as his brother and it was strange to see them together like this. For the first time, she could see the similarities in the slopes of their shoulders. She mistakenly thought because they were so different, that they weren't close but seeing them like this it was easy to see they were.

"Our last job was to infiltrate the house where some of the girls were being kept. The ones we rescued that are getting help, they've slowly, after a lot of therapy, begun to open up to us. We also found files that corroborate what we've been told."

"How can we help? Above what we're doing?"

Gideon looked determined, his jaw hardening with it, his gaze singularly focused on her.

"I'm going to put a call into my team. I think the time is right for me to bring them in on this and break it open."

"You're going to drop the undercover part?"

Either it was her overactive imagination or Gideon looked disappointed about that possibility. She didn't have any intention of trying to unpack the emotions that thought caused. "No, I don't think so, but I need to talk to my team and see how we move forward with things now that everything's gotten more complicated."

Gideon nodded, his brows slashed low on his forehead, and she gave him what she hoped was a reassuring smile.

She laid a hand on his arm and felt the muscle bunch beneath her fingertips. "Don't worry, we'll figure this out. My team are the best there is at this kind of thing."

"I need to make a few calls." Damon stood abruptly and left the penthouse, his strides angry. She knew he was in pain from the revelations that had been necessary today. Gideon's eyes came to hers and she saw the shuttered emotion fighting to break out and it caused her heart to beat wildly in her chest.

"This is a dangerous job, isn't it? What you do?"

It was as if he was just figuring out that she wasn't the personal assistant he'd tortured for months, and he didn't like the thought.

Duchess didn't want to confirm his obvious fears and open the door to her own self-doubts. "We're good at what we do."

"Do people ever get hurt?"

Rolling her lips over her teeth, she thought about Snow getting shot and the close call with the bomb Reaper and Hurricane had to defuse, and then Charlie almost dying, and hated it. Gideon was watching her, waiting for her reply as if he didn't already know the answer, and she didn't know what he wanted from her. Of course it was dangerous, and people got hurt and worse but that was who she was.

"Just promise me you'll be careful, okay? I know you're some kind of badass warrior but you're…" He stopped and Duchess felt like her breath froze in her chest. His eyes tracked her from head to foot as if he was seeing her for the first time and she could read the look in them. "Just be careful."

His hand dropped and she let out a whoosh of pent-up air from her lungs. "Always am."

She stepped away and wondered what had just happened between them. He'd wanted to say more, and she had the sudden itch to show him who she was without the walls she kept up for her own protection. His eyes were on her as she left the room, needing the space to get herself under control, so she didn't blurt out something she shouldn't. Pulling her phone from her bag, she hit dial on the number of the person she knew would pull her head back into this deadly game.

"Bás."

"I need a secure line."

She heard him switch and move on the other end and let out a breath. This was where she felt confident, felt sure. Even fighting with Gideon, she was in control. Him showing her the softer side of his personality, now and when she was sick, made her wary. She knew that opening up like that came with the real possibility of getting hurt in a way she found more dangerous than any bullet.

CHAPTER 8

Gideon paced the length of his living room, his hand rubbing at the back of his neck as he waited for some of Nadia's team to arrive so they could formulate a plan. How could he have been so blind, so naive to what was really happening around him? His half-brother exacting such atrocious things on innocent women was a hard pill to swallow. He himself may have been cool, even cold with the women he'd spent time with, but none could say he'd forced or coerced them in any way. That they had the same father was shameful to him and he'd been struggling with that, among other things, since Nadia had laid it all out for him and Damon.

Today had been one of revelations, discovering his brother was a murdering sexual predator was a difficult thing to wrap his head around. He'd known Carter was a bad apple but what he'd learned today caused a pit to swim in his stomach. That he'd tried to implicate him in some way made hot and thick fury curl in his belly until he was almost choking on it.

After the call to her team, Nadia convinced him and Damon to go back to their offices and act as normal as possible to anyone watching. He'd been against it; not sure he'd be able to keep the lid on his chaotic emotions and the anger surging through him like a wild animal on the prowl.

He'd done as she'd said though because, deep down, he knew it was the right move, and because, for the first time, he was seeing her for who she really was. Not a woman he was attracted to so badly that he became a raging asshole to try and deflect it. Not as his PA who he worked to the bone in an effort to punish her for making him want her so badly. No, he finally saw her for who she was, a warrior fighting a battle unseen to the masses. A woman willing to fight for those who couldn't fight for themselves, even if it meant putting herself on the line. It made him want her more, but worse, it made a crack open in his chest as if suddenly the organ was too big for the space it assumed. In the space of ten hours, he'd felt his entire demeanour shift in regard to Nadia.

She'd calmed him when he'd been ready to go and find Carter and rip him apart for what he'd done. She'd kept him busy with meetings all afternoon so he couldn't focus on the shit going on in his life and she'd delivered the news with clear concise compassion and honesty when he knew she could have lied.

He wished this new version of Nadia he was seeing, who he'd already been desperate for, would make him want her less. But wasn't it his shitty luck that he only wanted her more now? He wanted to unwrap each of her delicious layers and expose her secrets one at a time.

"You need to calm down."

His eyes moved to where she was looking out into the night sky, her arms crossed over her chest. She'd changed into dark skin-tight jeans and a black, long-sleeve tee which clung to her curves, teasing him until he was half mad.

She was magnificent as she waited silently, her eyes on the skyline, an air of calm he certainly didn't feel winding around her. Need, sharp and savage, laced up his spine and he had the overwhelming urge to reach out and touch her.

Moving closer, he shoved his hands in his pockets to help him resist the urge so potent in his veins. "How do you do it?"

She didn't pretend to misunderstand what he was asking, and it was one more thing he liked about her. Women in the past had been entertaining, but they'd all wanted a piece of him and used manipulation to try and get their claws into him. It was the reason he'd never let any of them close or stopped to really see past the cunning they thought to hide. Not until this woman had cut down his defences like they were made of the finest silk.

"I don't always. It's like anything, the longer you do it the easier it gets, but…"

She stopped and he turned his body so he was facing her as she kept her body to the glass. Her head was high, chin proud, but he saw a moment of vulnerability in the exhale before she smiled and turned to him. "But?"

"There are always the cases that slip past your defences and become more personal."

"Is this one of those cases?"

He was almost holding his breath as he waited for her answer. He stepped closer until her arm was brushing his chest and the room felt charged with tension, some of it sexual for sure. But it was more than just sex, it was something he wasn't sure he wanted to define. He just knew that this woman was important to him in a way that could change his life. It terrified him but he had the urge to lean into it instead of fighting it as he'd been these last months. To let things happen and see where they ended up.

"Yes."

He was about to ask her in what way it was different but the sound of the elevator announcing a visitor had them both snapping out of the little bubble of truth they'd shared.

Nadia gave him a searching look filled with heat and something he couldn't define before she moved from the window to greet her people. He followed, his eyes glued to the beautiful woman who was so dangerous to him.

Watching her in his space seemed natural as if she belonged there and he found he wanted her to stay. She warmed the cold spots of his penthouse, lighting them with a sense of home.

Stepping forward, he dropped his shoulders, lifting his chin as four men and a woman came into view. Nadia greeted them warmly, openly, and he saw true affection move between the group. Something he'd never really had, either at work or at home, at least not since his mother died.

"Gideon, I'd like you to meet the team and my friends."

Her smile was small as she stepped beside him, planting herself in his court and it felt significant to him that she did it. Although maybe he was reading into things that weren't there in an effort to make up for how blind he'd been.

"Nice to meet you."

Nadia motioned to the first man. "This is Bás, my boss."

The man was tall and broad, with an air of 'I will hunt you down and kill you if you so much as breath at me wrong'. He was intimidating as fuck and that was from someone who was always considered the one to be wary of.

"Don't listen to her, she's the one who keeps us in line."

His accent had an Irish lilt that was mellow but there in the way he said his D's making them sound almost like a J.

Nadia snorted and then moved on to the next man. "This is Hurricane. He's been in London the last few days watching my six."

All of these men were huge but this guy was next level. This man had the shoulders of a linebacker, black skin, and hair cut close to his skull. He looked like he could crush you with one big fist but when he reached forward to shake Gideon's hand, his grin was warm and sincere, and Gideon had the feeling he was a big teddy bear.

"Good to meet you, Gideon."

"Likewise."

"This is Titan."

Titan was a good name for him. He was tall, his skin black but not as dark as Hurricane's, but his nod in greeting was more watchful than the other two men so far. Gideon got the feeling he was sizing him up before making a judgment.

Gideon nodded back, letting them lead the introductions and size him up as he was them.

"Next up is Lotus. Don't take any notice of her sharp tongue. She's a pussy cat."

He looked at the petite woman with dark hair and a face made for the cover of a magazine and knew without a doubt she'd be the one to take him down if he so much as stepped out of line.

"If by pussy cat you mean sleek panther, then yeah, that's me."

Gideon smiled as he took her hand. Her grip was firm and no-nonsense as was the look she gave him. "Nice to meet you, Lotus."

"Lastly and by no means least, is Reaper."

"Hell, are all your names meant to scare the crap out of people?"

Reaper laughed as he leaned forward to shake his hand. "Ha, I wish that were the case, mate, but usually it's for other reasons. The scary shit is a bonus."

"An Aussie."

"Yep, sure am."

"I spent a summer there when I was a teen. It's the most beautiful place on earth."

Reaper's smile was wide. "It sure is."

"Right, that's enough with the introductions. Let's get down to business."

Gideon nodded at Nadia as she led them into his living room as if it were her own. The large space looked dwarfed as the seven of them sat or stood in different places around the room. Lotus produced a laptop from her bag and opened the screen before clicking on some buttons.

"I'm pulling Watchdog and Bein in via video link."

It was strange to feel like a guest in his own home but the way they took control seemed natural to them. To him, who'd always needed his own control, it was difficult to let go. It left him feeling surplus to requirements and he didn't like it.

As the screen filled, he saw another two men. Again, they both looked like they chewed nails for breakfast.

"Did you know that Koala fingerprints are almost indistinguishable from a human's, so much so, they can confuse a crime scene and ruin a case?"

Nadia laughed but nobody seemed shocked by the man's opening statement.

"This is Watchdog, our resident tech genius and fact procurer."

"I think you mean overall genius."

"Fine, an overall genius with an IQ score that looks like it is in fact the measurement of his big, fat head."

Reaper snorted and Lotus belly laughed, giving him a glimpse at the true dynamics of this team.

"Cut the shit, we have work to do." At Bás' tone they all quit laughing and he turned to Nadia. "Duchess, update please."

"Well as you know, Gideon's father reached out wanting Carter to handle the Macey deal. Enough that he threatened to have Gideon fired if he said no, which shows us how much Carter wants this to happen. We found bugs in this property, but none have ever been found in the offices."

Reaper sat forward. "Did you destroy them all?"

"No." Nadia reached for her bag and produced the tiny bug, handing it over to the blond man.

He turned it over in his hand and squinted before nodding. "I'll get this over to Bishop but I'm pretty sure this is what SIS is using."

"SIS?" Gideon was getting lost already and a headache was forming behind his eyes as if things were spiralling out of his grasp.

"SIS is what we call MI5 and MI6. It's what they're known as now," Bás informed him as if he should already know this.

"It's not."

Gideon blinked at Nadia's sharp tone.

All eyes turned to her and Bás cocked his head in question. "What's not?"

"The bug isn't an SIS-approved brand, at least not anymore."

"You spoke to a contact there?"

"Kind of. I have a CI that gives me tidbits sometimes and she told me a few months back that SIS had switched distributors for their equipment because of a cost issue. They stopped contracting with the company that makes those ones about a year ago."

He felt his heart quicken watching her in this role. Although today had been the first time he'd seen this side of her, watching more of her unfold was disconcerting and a little bit arousing.

"So, you don't think Carter or Project Cradle has someone inside MI6?"

Gideon glanced at Hurricane as he asked Nadia and it felt surreal to even be having this conversation.

"It wouldn't shock me. We all know there are some real assholes in both agencies as well as the good people."

"Yeah, except the good ones quit."

Nadia smiled at Bás. "Well, good for you that I did or you'd be wrangling these assholes on your own."

"Hey, who are you calling an asshole?" Titan winked at Duchess who laughed.

"Wait, you were MI6?"

Nadia glanced at him and nodded. "Yes, before this job I was."

"Okay then." He wanted to say so much more but shut his mouth so he didn't look like a bigger idiot in front of these people.

Hurricane slapped him on the shoulder. "It's okay, man. We're a lot to handle, especially these two." He pointed at Lotus and Reaper who flipped him off.

"Focus," Bás snapped as he rubbed the spot between his eyes, frustration creeping into his features.

"What else do we know?"

Gideon listened as the team reeled off everything they knew so far and for a slight moment he worried that they were being so forthright in front of him. Was he going to end up in a body bag at some stage to keep these secrets? He knew this team were secret and that they were linked to the team who initially contacted him, Eidolon or something, but he didn't know who they worked for or the details. Just that he'd signed a stringent NDA when they began the work.

A hand landed on his arm, and he fought the instinctive flinch.

"You, okay?"

"Yeah, just trying to take it all in and process it."

Nadia tilted her head, and he had the almost overwhelming desire to sink his teeth into the soft delicate skin of her neck and mark her.

"It's a lot to deal with but if you have any questions, just ask. They don't bite, honest." Her eyes warmed and it took everything in him not to pick her up and take her to his bed, fuck this, fuck Carter, fuck his father. All he wanted was a night to lose himself in her body.

"We do bite, so you might want to lay off the fuck-me eyes, buddy."

Gideon blinked, pulling his gaze away from Nadia who was blushing and looking at Lotus with a thunderous expression. She had a smart mouth and a chip on her shoulder the size of the Grand Canyon.

Nadia went to respond "Lotus...."

He held up his hand to stop her. Leaning forward he looked Lotus directly in the eye. "And you might want to remember you're in my home. I might not be the person with all the answers or even have any control over what the fuck is happening in my life right now, but you'll show me some respect in my own home, or you can show yourself out."

Lotus looked like she wanted to castrate him with a blunt fork, but Gideon held her stare, not flinching or backing down and the room fell silent. So silent he could've heard a flea fart it was so quiet, and he wondered if he'd just signed his own death warrant.

"Point taken. I apologize if I was out of line."

It looked like her jaw might crack from the effort as she spoke through her teeth as if she wanted to drag the words back. "If?"

Lotus sighed. "Fine, I was out of line, but this," she pointed around her, "this is my family and I'm just looking out for Duchess."

"I get that, but there's no need. I'd never hurt her, and anyway, it isn't like that." He lied through his teeth because he wanted to be that and every person in the room knew it, except for perhaps Nadia.

Hurricane snorted. "Yeah okay."

"Would you like Lotus to leave?"

Gideon turned to Bás who was watching him with no obvious expression indicating his thoughts on the last few minute's interactions.

"No, it was a misunderstanding. I just want my life back, and Carter and this whole hideous nightmare to end."

"Let's formulate a plan to make that happen."

"We need to get to Carter and Marsha, that's the goal. We should plant some hardware of our own."

"Carter is having a black-tie ball at his home a week on Friday. Damon and I always get an invite. We don't go but we always get the invite to go."

Hurricane nodded and Gideon found himself liking the man more and more.

"You should both go."

"We can't send them in alone and expect them to plant the bugs." Lotus shrugged.

"Lotus and I should go as their dates. If we can distract him, it might give you guys time to get in and see if you can find anything useful. Carter already believes Gideon and I are dating so it wouldn't be that much of a stretch for me to go with him, and Damon is known for his beautiful dates."

He knew it was her job, but it didn't stop the instinctive desire to want to keep Nadia as far away from Carter as he could. He rolled his lips between his teeth in an effort to keep the words from slipping out.

"That's a great idea, and in the meantime, Watchdog can do a deep dive into Macey. There has to be a reason Carter wants this deal and we need to find out what it is."

"I already found a link." Watchdog remarked.

Everyone turned to the computer monitor and Gideon let out a breath now that the urge to flat-out refuse the plan to go to the damn stupid party passed somewhat.

"Well?" Bás asked throwing his hands up as Watchdog just looked at them.

"Oh, yeah, sorry. So, the owner of Macey's is Tarquin Green. He's old Texas money. His oldest son is set to take over Macey's at the start of the next financial quarter. Turns out he ran in the same circles as Marsha when they were kids before she changed her name."

"That makes sense, but we need more than that."

"Let me finish. Tarquin has a daughter, Melissa, who'd fit the timeline for when Marsha went into the facility."

Gideon leaned forward. "You think the daughter, Melissa, is the one Marsha gave birth to?"

Watchdog nodded and turned to Bein to continue. "Snow and I have been doing some digging and Melissa's birth certificate says his first wife is the mother but that's impossible. He didn't meet her until Melissa was almost two months old. There is also a strong resemblance to Marsha."

An image popped onto the screen and Gideon sucked in a breath at the sight of the woman who was the spitting image of the one who was ruining his life.

"Holy shit!" Reaper exclaimed.

"Yeah, that's what we thought. I think it's entirely plausible she's Marsha and Tarquin's daughter. We just have no clue how he ended up with her in his care and what his involvement is with Project Cradle now."

"Bein, you and Val head to Texas and dig in. Find out whatever you can. Perhaps stage a meeting with Melissa and get us some DNA so we can confirm our theory."

"Will do, boss."

Bás turned to the rest of them. "We should leave you in place if your cover is still good, Duchess. But maybe play up the attraction between you and be seen out so Carter buys you as his date. That motherfucker is suspicious so, Lotus, you'll need to do the same with Damon."

He pinned Gideon with a gaze. "You think you can get Damon on board with this?"

He nodded. "Yes, he wants this over as much as I do."

"Good."

Bás shoved his hands into the pockets of his leather jacket. "Call your dad and tell him you'll do as he asks, but that you want to meet with Carter at your office to discuss it first. When Carter arrives, tell him you want in on whatever deal he's making."

Gideon began to pace, shaking his head as his skin itched with the desire to deny Carter anything.

A hand landed on his forearm, and he stilled looking up to see Nadia watching him.

"Talk to me."

Gideon glanced up to see the rest of the team had retreated onto his terrace to give them privacy. "I hate this. I just want to rip him to shreds and I don't know if I can do this without letting that show."

Nadia pulled him toward the couch and sat, pulling him down beside her and he went like an eager puppy, proving how much this woman was under his skin.

"Do you remember when we first met?"

He blinked and his mind went to the first time he'd laid eyes on her and the visceral reaction he'd had and how it had taken everything in him to not thread his hands through her hair and splay her on the top of his conference table like a feast.

"Yes."

"Do you remember what you said to me?"

"I said you looked like a mouse who wouldn't be able to hack it."

Nadia chuckled and it made his heart squeeze like a vice. "Yes, you did. Do you remember what I said back?"

"That what I said was perfect because that was the look you were going for."

"Yes, I did say that, and it was true. I also knew in that second that you hated me."

He took her hand and lifted it to his lips, running the tips along his cheek. "I never hated you. I wanted you and I hated it."

"But I didn't know. You hid it so well I believed you and you need to channel whatever that was again so we can end this for you and Damon."

"I'm sorry." Gideon ran his thumb over her bottom lip, wanting to kiss her more than his next breath.

"It's fine."

"It's not. I've been a raging asshole to you when all you were trying to do was help us. The truth is I like you, Nadia. I didn't expect that or foresee it and I don't do well with surprises or emotions out of my control or comfort zone."

"I like you too, as proved by my dry-humping you earlier."

Gideon let out a loud laugh as the moment lightened. "You never say what I think you're going to."

"More surprises. I must be your worst nightmare."

"Hmm, more like my biggest fantasy right now."

"Well, you need to table that for now and call your dad and meet with Carter."

"Will you be with me during the meeting?"

"Do you want me there?"

Gideon nodded. "Yes, you calm me." Her features softened and he had the overwhelming feeling that he could fall for this woman.

"Then I'll be there."

"Good, I'll let the others back in and we can get started."

Gideon turned and saw eyes on them and dropped his hand from her face.

"Great, Lotus is going to kick me in the balls."

"It's okay, I'll protect you."

He was about to respond when the flash of a red dot caught his eye and the next thing he knew, the world exploded around him.

CHAPTER 9

Duchess saw the dot a split second before the shot was fired and reacted, throwing her body across Gideon's and forcing them both to the floor between the coffee table and the couch, her body landing with a jolt against his. Shouted words of warning rang out as bullets pinged around them, the air ringing with the sound of glass shattering.

"Sniper."

Bás and Hurricane dove behind the outdoor furniture for cover, their instincts kicking in a split second later, as she tried to raise her head and figure out what was happening without getting shot. Lotus and Reaper made it just inside the door and used the column of the walls as cover. Titan was pinned down by the outer wall as they all tried to figure out where the shooter was.

"Reaper, Lotus, get over to the building across the street. I think he has a nest there. Duchess, get Gideon away from any windows."

As Bás and Hurricane returned fire, Lotus and Reaper ran from the room, heading to try and take out the sniper that had them pinned. Duchess gripped Gideon's shirt and faced him.

"We need to move. Do exactly what I tell you, okay?"

He nodded, his eyes never leaving her and filled with a trust she'd never seen before.

"When I say run, I want you to stay low and get behind the island in the kitchen."

"Got it. What about you?"

Duchess pulled her sidearm out from the back of the black jeans she'd changed into and checked the clip. She nodded to Bás. "Give me some cover fire."

At once Hurricane, Titan—who'd managed to get himself into a better position—and Bás laid down fire.

"I'm right behind you. Go."

As Gideon scrambled on quick feet toward the kitchen, she and the team covered them and, as quick as it began, the attack stopped. Dragging in a breath, she ran her hands over Gideon checking him for a wound until he gripped her wrists and held her still.

"I'm fine, Nadia."

A shaky feeling she'd never had after an attack like that made her chest feel tight. Until he wrapped her in his arms and held her against his body and she could feel the fast, reassuring pounding of his heart against her own. His lips against her hair made her want to sob and that was a new reaction too.

Blinking fast, she swallowed and tried to get her emotions under control. She wasn't by nature an overly emotional person, but she accepted, if only to herself, that Gideon was different.

"Are you okay?"

She nodded as she felt his lips against her hair, his arms tight around her.

A shadow fell over them and she pulled out of his hold and hauled herself to her feet, putting some space between her and Gideon as she looked at Bás.

"You both good?"

Duchess nodded. "Yeah, we're fine. Is everyone else okay?"

"Yeah, but we need to go. It's not safe here and there'll be more coming."

Duchess turned to Gideon. "Grab what you can't live without, but not your phone or any electricals."

Gideon took off and Titan followed him with a nod to her. She knew Titan would make sure he only packed what he needed and was quick. When she was sure he was out of hearing range, she turned to Bás. His brow was slashed low, his jaw locked tight, and anger and energy emanated from every pore.

"This is escalating."

"I know and I can't help thinking it's because we're getting too close to the head of the snake."

Duchess inclined her head. "Hansen?"

Joel Hansen was the man who'd started this manhunt and exposed the network. He was ex-CIA and had been a handler for two of the Eidolon women. Sisters who'd been his assets. He'd treated them both abhorrently and had gotten one pregnant and then left her to die when her undercover job went sideways. There was more though, a deep-seated hatred between him and Bás that went back further.

She hadn't pushed for answers from her boss and friend because everyone had a past, especially in this team, but it was becoming apparent that they'd need to talk, and soon.

"Perhaps."

"We need to bring the entire team in on this and you need to tell us whatever it is you've been holding back."

Bás grasped the back of his neck and sighed. "I know but let's get somewhere safe first."

"Where are you thinking?"

"The place in Farnham. We can get there quickly, and Watchdog can make sure we aren't followed using the cameras on the motorways."

"Agreed."

She lifted her head to watch Gideon walking down the hall, a bag over his shoulder and Titan shadowing him. Before she could speak,

Bás' phone rang, and he answered, putting it on speaker. "Talk to me, Reaper."

"Found the nest but no sign of the shooter."

"Anything useful?"

"Nothing I can see. He must have done his homework though because this is a disused office and has a direct line of sight to Gideon's living room."

"Get what you need and meet us at safe house five."

"Roger that."

Duchess knew Bás was being cautious by not revealing the location in front of Gideon and the truth was, they'd probably have to blindfold him for the journey to keep the location safe for him and them.

Reaper hung up and Gideon stepped forward, worry etched on his face as he moved into her space, his masculine scent making it difficult to concentrate.

"Is Damon safe?"

"I'll have Reaper and Lotus pick him up on their way to the safe house."

Gideon blew out a breath of air, ruffling the fine hair on her neck as he did, and she fought her reaction to him.

"Thank you. What about the call to my dad?"

"We can handle that when we get to our destination."

"Let's get out of here."

They headed down in the lift but instead of taking the front exit, they left through the side, with Hurricane, who'd been unusually quiet, flanking Gideon on the other side to Titan. She and Bás covered the front and rear.

"We're clear."

They climbed into the blacked-out Land Rover that was a few years old and a little beat up so as not to draw the attention of a new model. She slid in beside Gideon in the back. Bás jumped into the driver's seat with Titan beside him and Hurricane took the seat on the other side of Gideon, basically caging him between them.

As Bás gunned the engine, she caught the look he gave Hurricane and clenched her jaw. Hurricane turned to Gideon who was tapping his fingers on his knee in agitation, and she laid her hand over his to reassure him.

"Sorry, buddy."

Gideon turned to Hurricane as he spoke, and she watched her friend stick the man she was coming to care for with a needle. Before his shock and betrayal could be voiced, he was out cold. His body slumped against her.

"That was a dick move."

"You know the score, Duchess. We can't take any chances and there are still questions to be answered that he can't help us with."

"He isn't involved in this."

Hurricane looked away, leaving Bás to take up this one. His eyes bored into hers, seeking answers to questions he wasn't voicing aloud.

"Maybe but until we're sure, we have no choice."

Duchess glared at him, even knowing he was right, but they could have gone about it better.

"There's always a choice, Bás."

"Maybe but sometimes all the options are shitty, and you just have to pick the one you think is the best and hope it doesn't backfire on you."

The car was silent the rest of the drive, except for a text from Lotus to the group confirming they had Damon and were headed their way and about an hour behind them.

Duchess felt exhaustion pulling at her but was too wired to sleep. She needed answers and right now the biggest one was what the hell was she going to do about this attraction between her and Gideon.

She knew other members of the team had met their partners on the job and made it work. Bein and Aoife had met when the barmaid had been hiding from her father, the King of the Irish mafia. It had worked out well for them in the end despite some hairy moments and they were happy and building a life. Same for Snow and Sebastian, the Judge she'd been undercover with. They were married and adding a baby to their family. Then there was Reaper and Princess Lucía, a bona fide Spanish Princess, her father was the King of Spain and they'd found a way too.

Even Charlie and Bishop, a couple who'd been through absolute hell to get where they were now were making it work. Her heart clenched at the love she saw between all those couples, and she'd be lying if she said she didn't want the same. For a man to look at her as if she was the sole purpose he breathed air.

The questions, among so many others rattling around her brain, was could she take the chance on it? Did she want to and did Gideon even feel the same? He wanted her, that was clear from day one but did he want more? She just didn't know, and perhaps now was the wrong time but she couldn't seem to compartmentalise like she had on other missions.

Arriving at the safe house, Bás and Titan cleared it before she eased herself out of the vehicle and stepped back, allowing Hurricane to lift Gideon over his shoulder and carry him inside. The house was a four-bedroom farmhouse with acres of land around it, giving them the privacy they needed. To anyone looking, it looked abandoned, but inside was a different story.

Each door and window was fortified, it also had a weapons and comms room, and a fully stocked kitchen with everything they'd need to survive for a prolonged period. Not that she thought they'd be here long at all.

Following Hurricane down the hallway and up the stairs, she rushed to open the door so Hurricane didn't bounce Gideon's head off it.

"Watch his head, dumbass." Hurricane smirked at her and she rolled her eyes. "Shut up."

"What? I'm happy for you."

Hurricane placed Gideon on the bed, and she bent over, making sure he was comfortable and checking his pulse. It beat strong beneath her fingers, his skin warm and her heart skipped at the feeling of home he gave her even now when he was unaware of everything.

"I don't know what you're talking about." She almost winced at her haughty tone, which was a dead giveaway.

"Sure you don't."

Duchess locked eyes with Hurricane, turning her body and crossing her arms over her chest. "It's nothing. You heard him."

Her friend tilted his head, his eyes focused on her as he folded his arms across his chest, mirroring her. "We all know the biggest lies are the ones we don't voice, Duchess. He may have said that but not a person in that room believed it and neither do you. Just be careful. He seems like a good guy, but we all know people hide shit and we still have a question mark over his involvement."

"He isn't involved in this." Her staunch denial was swift, but she knew in her heart it was true. Gideon was being used as a fall guy in some way. She didn't know how, just that it was happening.

"I hope not, Duchess. I like him for you, and you deserve to be happy."

"You're getting way ahead of yourself, Hurricane."

"Maybe, maybe not."

She wasn't usually candid about her feelings, even to the people who meant the most to her in the world, but she found herself wanting reassurance that she wasn't sure anyone could give her. "What if it all goes wrong? What if this is just lust caused by the circumstances we're in at the moment?"

"Listen, Duchess, I'm not an expert by any stretch of the imagination, but I do know this. Life is about risk, and putting your heart on the line is the biggest of them all, but it also has the biggest payoff."

"You sound like you know something about it."

The man in front of her looked sad, lost, and, not for the first time, she wondered what was going on with him and vowed to get to the bottom of it.

Hurricane blinked, dropping his head, and when he looked back up the intensity from seconds before was masked behind a wall of a smile. "Nah, just been forced to watch too many romantic comedies with my cousin growing up."

Duchess smirked but was stopped from responding by the sound of a groan behind her. Spinning, she dropped to her knees beside the man on the bed who was consuming her thoughts more and more. "Gideon, it's okay. You're safe."

His sluggish head lifted, drugged eyes trying to focus and make sense of what was happening to him. He'd come around quicker than she expected but she was glad for it. She didn't like seeing such a vital strong man weak.

Gideon swung his big body up, planting his feet on the ground, as he swayed, his head in his hands, his hair tousled, giving him the look of a younger man, not the titan that he was in the boardroom.

"Where are we?"

"Safe."

His body tensed and the next second he was lunging towards Hurricane. His legs gave way and, as he swung for Hurricane, her friend caught him and helped him stand.

"Steady on, buddy. You ain't ready for a fight just yet. Let the drugs move out of your body and then you can take a swing at me, okay?"

"Motherfucker drugged me."

His accusing eyes landed on her, and she fought the flinch and the look of betrayal in his eyes. "We had no choice. We can't let you know where we are for your safety and ours."

"You could've just said that."

Duchess rested her hands on his chest as she felt Hurricane leave the room.

"I know and we should have. I'm sorry."

A grunt was his only reply before he let his body sink back onto the bed, his legs too weak to hold him up. Duchess sat beside him silently, wondering what she could say. This was a messed-up situation to be sure.

His hand covered hers and he twined their fingers together before pulling their joined hands to his lips. His warm breath feathered over her skin causing goosebumps to break out all over her body. "Don't shut me out. I know you need to keep your secrets to be safe and I want that, but just talk to me. I like you, Duchess, and I want to get to know you better. Not as my PA or as a secret agent spy or whatever the hell you call yourself, but you, the person who loves tattoos of flowers and fights for the underdog."

"I want that too, but is now the right time?"

"Probably not, but what I'm learning is that life doesn't always give us the things we want when we want them, but she does give us the things we need. Let's seize the day and see what happens?"

He'd dropped their hands to his lap and turned his body into hers. His gaze was earnest and pleading and she knew this wasn't a man who begged for anything, especially not someone's time or attention. He was making himself vulnerable to her and she needed to decide if she was brave enough to do the same.

"What if I'm not enough? What if you hurt me?"

He leaned his forehead against hers. "I'll never knowingly hurt you, Nadia. I'd never take a gift like that and treat it with anything other than the utmost care and respect."

She wanted to believe him, but fear held her silent, her heart beating rapidly in her chest.

Gideon sighed and dropped a kiss on her temple. "It's okay, I can be patient. I'll wait. I just ask that you give it a chance and not shut me or the chance of something between us down."

Duchess nodded. "I can do that."

"Thank you."

He tipped her chin back with his finger and lightly kissed her lips. It wasn't dark and demanding like his previous kisses, it was light and tender and absolutely devastating to her resolve. Tears pricked her eyelids with the emotion that one kiss could evoke.

Could she be brave? She wanted to be and maybe that was enough for now.

CHAPTER 10

It took a lot to rattle him, but the last twenty-four hours had shaken him to his core. Everything had changed. He'd changed, and it wasn't just the effects of the drugs Hurricane had shot into his system. He glared at the man from his place on the couch, and the guy just smirked and shrugged his shoulders.

On some level, Gideon understood why they'd done it, but it only amplified how out of control his life was and how much of an outsider he was in this tight-knit group. It wasn't a feeling he liked, especially where Nadia was concerned. It had felt like just the two of them in this dance at the office but it was clear now she had a world he wasn't a part of and he didn't like it.

His gaze was drawn to her, where she was leaning over behind Bás who was looking at something on a laptop.

"She likes you."

Gideon glanced up as Titan came to sit beside him. They hadn't really spoken but he got the sense he was well-liked in the group from the interactions he'd witnessed. His attention was pulled back to Nadia as she laughed at something and then looked toward him. As if she too needed to keep checking he was safe. He saw the heat in her gaze, the way her eyes would drink him in like a thirsty person in the desert.

"I like her too." He had no intention of giving his innermost thoughts away, but he knew these people were looking out for her and, although grudgingly, he respected that.

"I was in a London gang before I joined Shadow."

Gideon dragged his attention from Nadia, turning to face Titan, as he had a feeling the man didn't give this kind of information away to just anyone, and there was a purpose for him doing it now.

"Yeah, I thought I detected an accent."

"You heard of the Cobras?"

Gideon shook his head and then stopped. "I heard something on the news a few years back but can't remember the details."

Titan nodded and then looked back toward Bás and Nadia. "I was the leader, and I did things that fill me with shame and regret. I betrayed my oldest friend. I kidnapped his woman and child. It almost killed me, and I mean literally and figuratively."

"Wow, that's not pretty."

Titan shook his head. "No, it's not. I had my reasons, but they weren't good enough to justify what I'd become." Titan sighed. "What I'm trying to say is this team, these people, they take the ugly parts of you and shape them into something more. A man who barely knew me gave me a second chance to redeem myself and payback for what I did, instead of being locked away behind bars where I should have been. Duchess is a big part of the man I am now. She showed me who I could be, and what I could achieve."

"Why are you telling me this?"

Titan turned and pinned him with a hard stare. "Because she's family to me. A sister, and she has a whole group of men who are like brothers to her, and I wanted to warn you that if you get involved with her you need to mean it. She isn't some cheap fuck, or a random hookup. She's special and needs to be treated as such."

"I would never treat her that way." Gideon wanted to feel irritated at the implication, but he respected that Titan voiced his thoughts and that she had people like him at her back.

"Good because if you hurt her, they won't find your body."

Gideon smirked until he realised the man was deadly serious and then lifted his chin and met his eye. This man was being honest, and he would too. "I've never met anyone like her before. She's smart, sexy, strong, but despite her sass and beauty, she has a vulnerability that she tries to hide. I want Nadia to show me that. I want to know her, who she is when the action stops, what her dreams are, what drives her to do this job, to fight for people she'll never know. She's special and I have a feeling if she asked me to lay my heart on a slab for her I'd do it and it's terrifying. More so than any threat you could make to me. So, I appreciate the warning, but I can promise you, I have no intention of hurting her."

Titan kept his eyes on him and then nodded. "That's all we want for her. She's a good person, one of the best, and she helped take a bunch of reprobates and shaped us into a team."

"She's amazing."

Gideon's gaze was pulled back to her as the door opened and Reaper and Lotus walked in with a haggard Damon behind them, a black cloth bag over his head.

Gideon leaned in towards Titan. "Honestly, I'm just glad the warning came from you and not Lotus. She scares the shit out of me."

Titan let out a loud belly laugh, his wide smile splitting his face and drawing attention from across the room. He stood and slapped a hand on his shoulder before looking down. "Oh, my friend, if you think you got away with it, you're sadly mistaken."

Gideon groaned. "For fuck's sake."

Titan walked away and he stood to move toward his brother, who was now blinking furiously after being in the dark.

"They put a hood over my head."

Gideon grinned despite the situation. "Count yourself lucky. They fucking knocked me out."

"Man, I thought we got past that?" Hurricane slapped a big arm over his shoulder and grinned.

Gideon gave him a cold look. "It'll take more than you letting me punch you to forgive that."

Hurricane held up his finger. "I have just the thing. When we get back to base, I'm gonna make my candied bacon for you." Hurricane made the chef's kiss motion with his hands. "It will change your life. My cousin Ashanti gave me the recipe when I visited her last year."

"Candied bacon?"

"Life changing."

A loud clap had them all turning in Bás' direction. "Enough with the cooking tips, this isn't fucking Bake Off. We have work to do."

"You watch Bake Off?"

Lotus seemed to zero in on what she thought was important information and totally ignored the scowl Bás aimed her way.

Gideon felt the brush of Nadia's hand on his arm as she stepped up next to him, his skin tingling in response to her.

Her smile was warm as she spoke. "She loves to rile him up."

"I watch it to relax me."

Gideon watched the leader of this fearless team blush a little.

Lotus smirked as she checked her nails. "Uh-huh."

"What the fuck does 'uh-huh' mean?"

"Nothing. I just know a certain someone loves that show."

"To be fair, Lotus, that isn't narrowing it down. Snow loves that show and so does Watchdog, not just Valentina."

Gideon gazed down at Nadia as she joined in with giving their boss shit.

"Who the fuck are these people?" Damon asked from beside him.

"The people who are going to save our ass and give us our lives back."

"I'm not having this conversation with you bunch of assholes, so pipe down."

"Fine but when you start piping flowers onto fairy cakes, we're having an intervention, boss man."

Bás pointed a finger at Lotus who looked totally unaffected by the glare he was giving her, in fact, she looked like she was enjoying pushing him. "You are a pain in my ass."

"Ah, thanks, boss. I love you too."

Bás shook his head and put his hands on his hips. "What the fuck did I do to deserve this shit?"

"You love us really."

"The fuck I do. Now, if we're finished can we focus? Gideon needs to make this call and we need to do recon and find out who sent that shooter after Gideon."

"Surely it's Carter?" Gideon was surprised there were even a doubt.

"We don't think so. He'd have nothing to gain by killing you."

Gideon felt his gut tighten. "Then who?"

"We think it's Marsha."

"Fuck."

"Yeah, but let's make the call and get the ball rolling. We want you to meet with him in your office and tell him you want in on this deal."

"If he says no?"

"He won't. The thought of corrupting you will play into his power games and he won't be able to resist. You can compound it by saying you and Damon are coming to the party and you want the family to work together. Make out you have financial issues."

"He'll check."

"And he'll find that the business, your apartment, and everything you own is mortgaged to the eyeballs."

Gideon felt his jaw fall before he gritted it. "Let me guess, the genius guy hacked my accounts?"

"Yeah, but don't worry, we'll give it back...." Lotus smirked at him. "Probably."

"Whatever, it's not like I have a choice."

Nadia rolled her lips between her teeth, and it took everything in him not to lean in and take a taste for himself.

"You have a choice, Gideon. We can find another way."

He ran his fingers along her arm, needing to touch her more than air. "Is this the best way?"

Her nod was slight, but he saw it and heard the sigh she let out. "Then let's do it. I want this over so I can start living my life again." A tiny frown appeared between her brows and the urge to kiss it away filled him. "It'll be okay, Nadia."

It should feel strange for him to be reassuring the woman who'd thrown her body over his to protect him from a bullet. A memory that made his gut roil with nausea. Not because he was almost shot but because she could have been hurt protecting him and he'd never have forgiven himself.

"Set up the call, Reaper."

The moment between them was gone as everyone sprang into action, all of them knowing the role they had to play. Gideon sat at the large oak kitchen table where everything was set up so the call wouldn't be traced and felt her hand on his shoulder.

"You got this."

Gideon nodded and listened as the call rang through to his father.

"Son."

"Dad, I'm calling to say I accept your deal. Have Carter come to my office at noon tomorrow."

"He will want you to go to him."

Gideon could hear the hesitancy in his old man's voice and hated him for what he was forcing him to do, and yet he'd always love the father he'd been before Marsha had come on the scene.

"If he wants this, he'll come to me at noon tomorrow and you can tell him to come alone. I won't have my office and staff intimidated by his fucking entourage. Am I clear?"

"Carter doesn't travel without a guard. You know how important he is, he needs protection."

"The only thing he needs protection from is that viper you call a wife. You heard the terms. Meet them or I'll let you sink this company and me with it. The difference is I'll survive, will you?"

Silence met his outburst, and he felt a smidgen of guilt for his words but when he glanced at Damon, his brother nodded in agreement. Gideon needed to remember it wasn't just him they had hurt, it was Damon too.

"I'll make sure it happens, son."

"Dad?"

"Yes, son?"

"That's the last time you call me that. I'll do this but after this, I'm dead to you. Do you understand? I'll play nice in public, but I want nothing to do with a man who'd threaten one son for another."

"You don't understand."

"No, I don't, and I don't care to."

Gideon hung up and felt wrung out by the short conversation.

"You okay?"

He covered the hand Nadia had placed on his shoulder with his own and leaned his head toward her. "Yeah, it was past time."

The room was buzzing with conversation and plans being made and whether it was the after-effects of the drugs or the fact he'd been forced to face so much, he needed some space. "Can I go outside and get some fresh air?"

"Yes, of course. There's a beautiful pond at the bottom of the garden that looks out onto the fields. At this time of the morning it will be chilly though, so take a coat."

"God, is it morning already?"

"Yeah, it's been one hell of a twenty-four hours. Go have five minutes of peace and quiet."

"That sounds nice."

He couldn't resist leaning in and taking her lips when she tipped her head to him. She tasted sweet and spicy, exactly like the person she was in real life. When he pulled away from the kiss, which was in danger of going nuclear at any second, her eyes were hazy. It made his dick hard just imagining her looking at him like that when she was naked beneath him.

"Hurricane is making us some food. It won't be anything special, maybe breakfast sandwiches, but do you want me to put something aside for you?"

His hand skimmed her side as he drew her to his body and placed a kiss on her temple. "Do you always look after others?"

"We all have our roles to play, this is part of mine."

Gideon pulled away a little. "I don't want to be part of a role to you."

"You're not."

He saw it then, the fear she'd spoken of earlier. Someone had hurt this woman who was coming to mean everything to him. She felt the need to protect and nurture, and he guessed it was because she needed to be needed.

"Some food would be good."

"Any preference?"

Gideon shook his head. "Nah, I'm easy."

Nadia snorted and then looked shocked by it, and he laughed.

"Does that ladylike sound infer I am, in fact, not easy?"

"Gideon, you're the least easy person I have ever met. You sent me back to the deli three times in one day because they didn't get your order exactly perfect."

A lightness he hadn't expected after yesterday filled him at her teasing. "That's because I needed an excuse to keep you coming back into my office."

"I'm your PA, Gideon, you don't need an excuse."

His arms tightened around her, and he grinned, and she drew in a breath.

"That smile should come with a warning."

"Yeah, what would it say?"

She tipped her head and her lips switched. "Warning, underwear may spontaneously combust."

Gideon chuckled. "Did that just happen?"

"I thought you needed some air?"

"Changing the subject. Okay. Well, I did need air but turns out I just needed you after all."

Nadia swatted his arm and pulled away as Reaper walked past them with his phone to his ear, a grin aimed at them.

"Get some fresh air, it will help with the drugs and I'll bring some food out for us."

"Okay."

He watched her turn away and didn't want to let her go. He wasn't sure he'd ever want to see her walk away from him.

"Nadia!"

Her silky hair swung as she turned to him with a raised eyebrow. "Yes?"

"You were never just my PA."

Her eyes softened and she blushed, and he fell just a tiny bit more in love with the woman he'd sworn to resist.

CHAPTER 11

It had been hectic, and she was running on caffeine and adrenaline. Since the shooting last night, everything had sprung into hyperdrive. An urgency that hadn't been there before snapped at everyone's heels.

She and some of the team had travelled back to London with Gideon, who'd offered to wear the hood. For now, Damon was staying at the safe house with Lotus and Reaper while she and Gideon would be using her flat. Her cover was still in place, so it would make sense that they were there together should Carter spot them. They were, after all, playing the part of lovers.

Playing because they weren't lovers...yet. She wanted him with a desperation she'd never experienced but whereas before it had felt like a hate fuck to get him out of her system, somehow it was so much more now. He'd shown her the real man beneath the asshole cloak he wore, and she realised she liked him. More than that, she could easily fall for him and had been doing so for a while without even realising it was happening.

Her phone buzzed with a heads-up from Hurricane that Carter was on his way up and had two men with him. She should've known that asshole wouldn't follow the rules. Her eyes stayed on the lift as she sent a warning text to Gideon, who was waiting in his office.

After the moment they shared yesterday, she'd been pulled into planning and they hadn't had another minute alone. Probably just as well, as she needed to focus.

A thumbs-up emoji pinged, and she smiled to herself. He'd loosened up since opening up to her about his father's demands and finding the bugs.

The lift doors dinged, and she looked up as they opened, revealing Carter Cavendish and two men from his security team.

Duchess stood playing her role as PA extraordinaire. "Mr Cavendish, please follow me."

Carter was handsome, like Damon and Gideon but he had his mother's cheekbones and her cool, grey gaze. He also had the class of an alley cat but seemed to think he was a king. Those eyes raked her skin, and she would've shivered in disgust if she hadn't had more restraint. Men like him had been ogling her since she was fourteen and developed breasts. This man was scum and the sooner he was wiped from the earth, the better.

"Well, it's a delight to see you again, Nadia."

He stepped closer, pinning her beside her desk, and she played the role of meek and timid as best she could, without being too weak. It was about balance with a man like Carter. He had to think he was in charge but not that she was available to him. She wanted him to believe her weak, so he never saw her coming.

His hand lifted and he stroked her collarbone, and she closed her eyes so he wouldn't see the hatred or the almost overwhelming desire she had to break every finger in his hand.

"Gideon seems to have upped his game. It was a wise decision to steal you from Damon. Perhaps my coming here will be a more regular thing now I know what's on offer, or perhaps I'll take some time with the family PA."

His unspoken words were clear. He thought she'd fucked Damon and was now fucking Gideon and he wanted his pound of flesh too.

"Get your fucking hands off her before I rip them off and shove them down your throat."

Gideon. Her eyes flashed open at the harsh demand and Carter slowly dropped his hand from her.

"Apologies, brother, I wasn't aware she belonged to you."

"Well, she does, so don't fucking touch her again. In fact, don't even look at her."

Duchess wanted to jump in and stop Gideon from showing his hand like he was. He didn't realise it but he'd just put a bigger target on her back than was already there. Men like Carter would only see the challenge in the warning.

"You never did like to share your toys, brother."

She saw Gideon's jaw flex with barely controlled rage before he spoke. "Shall we get down to business? We're both busy men, Carter."

Gideon waited as Carter and the two men with him walked inside his huge office. He held his hand out for her to proceed him, and she heard the whispered apology he gave her. She nodded, perhaps he did realise what he'd done but it was out there now.

Carter settled in the seat opposite Gideon, who'd rounded his desk. She stood to his left and Carter's men stood near the doors, arms loose at their sides, guns evident by the bulge in their jackets.

"You have a nice gig here, Gideon."

The envy wasn't something she'd expected from Carter as he looked around.

"I like it."

"Father says you're going to allow me to lead the deal with Macey."

"Yes, but there are conditions."

Carter cocked his head to Gideon, and Duchess watched a tick in his jaw. He didn't like this. He was chafing to throw his weight around.

"And they are?"

"I want in on whatever kickback you're taking from this, and don't lie and tell me there isn't one. We both know you don't do anything unless it benefits you in some way."

Carter smirked and Duchess wanted to punch him in the face but that was more Lotus' style than hers.

"Are you sure you want your plaything around for this?" Carter eyed her again and Gideon stiffened.

"She isn't a toy. She's going to be my wife."

Shock spread over her at his pronouncement, and also a profound sense of longing, which she wouldn't unpack right now. She recovered quickly when he reached for her hand, letting Gideon pull her closer so she was standing at his back.

"A wife you say? Well, isn't that a development? I had no idea you were serious."

"It's been a whirlwind."

"In that case, let me be the first to congratulate you. Or does Damon already know?"

Duchess detected jealousy in Carter's tone and wondered if that was the root cause of the discord in this family, flamed by a socially climbing mother.

"You're the first."

"Well then, congratulations. We must host a party for you."

"We'll be attending the black-tie ball this year, that will be sufficient."

"You will?"

"Yes, Damon too. It's past time this family put the past behind us and moved on from tiny slights."

"I agree." Carter looked guarded again and she knew Gideon needed to dial back the happy family speech. He must have felt it too because he shifted slightly.

"Plus, a deal with Macey could be beneficial to us both and a solid stance would be a good look for the board."

Carter sneered. "That's more like it, Gideon. I thought you'd gone soft for a second there."

"Not soft, pragmatic."

"What is it you think I can help you with or bring you in on?"

"I know you have something on Tarquin Green."

Carter cocked his head. "What is it you think I have?"

"Really, Carter, you expect me to lay all my cards on the table when you won't reveal any?"

Carter frowned but then chuckled. "Well, you're right. I do have something and it will allow us to get the deal done at a fraction of the cost."

"I can see how that will help me but what's in it for you?"

"Access to their shipping routes and a legitimate transportation for the models we'll be moving around the world as part of the fashion house."

"Models?"

"Yes, I have a new batch that I believe will work well for us and it cuts the red tape. A fashion house is perfect."

Duchess hoped Bás was getting all this on his end. It wasn't an admission of all the horrid shit he'd done but it was a start. He clearly wanted access to Macey's because it would be perfect for cleaning the money and providing a legitimate cover for what they did.

"I always knew you were into drugs and guns but you're in the flesh trade now?"

Duchess tensed but didn't outwardly react. Gideon was pushing too hard, he needed to rein it back.

"How could you suggest such a thing? I prefer to think of it as a service for both the girls who need our help and the businessmen that want the company. It's all consensual and legal, Gideon, so don't get your knickers in a twist. You always were the strait-laced one. Everyone always thinks it's Damon, but you've always had a stick up your ass. Which begs the question, why now?"

Gideon flexed his fist out of sight under the desk and she knew the subtle slight had pissed him off. "I'm in somewhat of a spot with cash flow and this would help me."

"Hmm, I see. So now you want to dirty your hands?"

"No, just a slight bending of the rules."

"Cautious as always, Gideon."

"Nothing wrong with being careful, Carter."

"I agree."

Gideon cocked his head. "Is that why you had documents and fake footage of me going in and out of your underground casinos?"

Shit.

He was going off-script.

Carter looked toward her, and she kept her gaze on the back of Gideon's head.

"It never hurts to have a little leverage in the bank, Gideon."

"Even if it's fake as fuck?"

Gideon was showing his anger and that wasn't a bad thing, Carter would expect some kind of reaction, so she let this play out and trusted that Gideon knew his brother well enough to know how far to push.

"Real and fake are just perceptions, Gideon. Who can tell these days what's real and what's fake."

His eyes moved to her, sliding over her from top to bottom, his insinuation clear.

The air was thick with tension now, an ugly poison swirling around the room, making it hard to breathe.

Gideon slapped the desk and leaned forward. "I want a percentage of the takings from the girls and you can handle the deal."

Carter grinned like he'd just gotten away with the heist of the century, leaning back in his chair, leg crossed so his Italian loafer caught the light from the polished surface. "You're already getting the advantage of a cheap deal, why would I give you anything more?"

Gideon leaned forward and rested his arms on the desk, his fingers linked as if he was relaxed but she could feel the tension in his spine as her hand rested on his shoulder. "Because you owe me for trying to have me killed last night."

Carter's brows winged up and genuine shock showed on his face for a moment before he shut it down. "I have no idea what you are talking about."

Gideon stood pushing his chair back in anger. "Don't fucking lie to me. This meeting is over. If you can't agree, I'll continue this deal on my own."

"I'm not lying, Gideon. If I wanted you dead, my men wouldn't be incompetent enough to miss."

"Then who?"

"I have a thought, but I need to confirm before I can voice it aloud."

"You have until the black-tie ball and then I want an answer."

"And if I don't tell you?"

"Then I'll tank this deal and watch the company burn."

"You love this company. You'd never let it fall. Look at how you almost killed yourself to save it after Daddy dearest almost bankrupted us."

"I do love this company, but as it was pointed out to me recently, I can start again. I could walk away from this and into a seven-figure job within the hour. I'd survive, fuck, I'd be better off, and you and I both know it."

"You could come work for me. We'd make a great team, Gideon."

"I'd rather die than go into business with family ever again."

"Perhaps you see why I struck out on my own."

"On your own? Don't forget Mummy has her hand up your ass pulling the strings, Carter."

Carter went red, his jaw clenching and Duchess mentally prepared for shit to head south, fast.

"Don't assume to know what you're talking about, Gideon. As you said yourself, you've had nothing to do with my business and no clue what you're talking about."

"Perhaps."

Silence descended on the room, just the tick of an antique clock punctuating the passing of time. Gideon broke it. "So do we have a deal?"

"I'll give you ten percent of the transaction on each girl, but I handle the deal with Tarquin Green."

"What leverage do you have on him?"

Carter stood and buttoned his jacket. "Come to the black-tie ball both of you, and I'll show you."

"We'll be there. Damon and a date too."

Carter held out his hand and Gideon took it and she knew it cost him to play this role. "To new opportunities."

"To family."

Carter grinned and turned to her, leaning in to kiss her cheek. "A pleasure to see you again, sister. I hope you can forgive my earlier rudeness."

He was charming and she could see how women fell for his charms, but she wasn't a fool. "Of course."

Carter and his men swept from the room, and she stood beside Gideon as the lift doors closed on them. Titan and Bás would pick them up from here and hopefully they had time to tag the cars.

"I feel dirty."

Duchess leaned her head against Gideon's shoulder. "I know how you feel. You did great though."

"I put you in more danger. He knows you're important to me now and that puts you at risk. Carter won't think twice about using that to control me."

"It's fine I can handle him. You thought on your feet and that's a good thing."

She followed him back into his office when Bás texted to confirm they had picked up Carter's trail on the street. The door closed and his arms came around her, pulling her close to his body. His masculine scent and heat enveloped her and she pressed against him.

"I hate that I put you at risk."

"You didn't put me at risk. This is my job, Gideon."

"Is that all I am?"

LETHAL SALVATION

"No."

His lips crashed down on hers and this kiss was demanding and filled with heat. He forced her lips open, his tongue thrusting inside as his hips ground against her. His hardness pressed into her belly as he backed her against the door. Sliding her hands into his hair, she raked her fingernails across his scalp, and he moaned into her mouth, his hips thrusting against her in a delicious rhythm.

His hand moved up her ribs, slipping beneath the silken material as he cupped her breast, his thumb sweeping over the lace and torturing her peaked nipple. A whimper escaped her throat as the hand cupped her ass, dragging her leg over his hip, her skirt hitching higher as he rocked into her, his hard length teasing her clit and driving her higher. His fingers dug into the skin of her ass, his callouses rough against her softer skin.

"Are you wet for me?"

He gave her no time to answer before his hands were on her, his fingertip sliding along the edge of her underwear. He lifted her leg higher, getting closer as they tore at each other's clothes.

A phone ringing had her stilling and suddenly she remembered they weren't alone, the cameras her team had put in the room were giving everyone a live feed of them making out like horny teens.

"Shit. Cameras."

Gideon stilled, his hand gently lowering her leg as he breathed hard through his nose. His voice was low against her neck, his breath tickling her skin. "I want you so bad I can hardly function."

"I want you, too."

Gideon sighed as he stepped back, giving her space to straighten her clothes while maintaining a private space, his back sheltering her from the camera. His thumb traced her bottom lip, his eyes dilated with desire and adrenalin. "I'll wait for you, Nadia."

She loved the way he said her name, like a caress over her spine. Hardly anyone called her Nadia, not even her parents, not that she saw them often. He wasn't the man she'd thought he was, not the shallow playboy with a bad attitude. That man she could fuck and still keep her heart safe. This one had all the sexual charisma of the man she'd met but also the sweet side who'd held her hair while she was sick; that man was smashing down every defensive wall she had as if they were paper thin.

"We should get back to work."

Duchess slipped around him and headed back to her desk outside his office door. Grabbing her bag, she rushed for the ladies' room to fix her hair and make-up before the entire floor became aware of what had almost occurred.

Her phone rang again as she was coming out of the ladies' room and she answered it quickly. "Yes."

"We need to talk."

Duchess sighed and nodded even though Bás couldn't see her. "Where and when?"

"The coffee shop on the ground floor in twenty minutes."

"See you there." Duchess hung up and walked back to her desk where Gideon was waiting.

"You, okay?"

She nodded. "Yeah, I need to meet Bás for a little while."

"I know, he called me too."

Duchess reared back slightly surprised by that but shrugged. "Let's go then. Bás is a real stickler for timekeeping."

Gideon held out his hand. "After you."

She gave him a sassy smile. "Such a gentleman."

"Not really, I just want to ogle your ass."

A laugh burst from her throat and the tension from the meeting and the intense kiss afterward lifted.

There went another piece of that wall.

CHAPTER 12

Gideon hated lying to her but, as he followed her to the ground floor of the building and walked into the coffee shop, he was glad he was there. In fact, he wouldn't be anywhere else right now.

Bás stood as they walked in and he caught his eye knowing he had to give Nadia some bad news but not what it was. He'd stopped for a second when Bás had called to question as why he might want him here but then realised the man read people for a living so reading his feelings for Nadia would be a cakewalk.

"I ordered for you both."

Gideon sat opposite Bás forcing Nadia into the corner. She might be badass, but his instinct would always be to protect her. She winked at him, clearly aware of what he'd done and letting him know it.

Nadia sipped the iced tea and sighed in delight as her eyes closed. "I love this stuff." Placing it back on the table, she looked at Bás, her head tilted slightly in question. "So, spill it."

"I have some news."

She rolled her hand in a hurry-up gesture. "And?"

Bás looked uncomfortable but seemed to pull himself together.

"There is no easy way to say this, Duchess, but your mother died yesterday morning."

She drew in a sharp inhale and reached for his hand without thinking. Gideon took it and gave it a squeeze as the colour drained from her face. God, he hated seeing her so wounded and wished Bás had done this in private rather than at a packed coffee shop.

"How?"

"Italian police say she was hit by a car. She died instantly at the scene."

Her hand shook in his and he leaned closer to rub her back, wanting more than anything to take away her pain.

"If you need to go take some time off and head to Italy and deal with this, we can handle things here."

Duchess nodded absently, her mind clearly trying to process the loss of her mother. "Thank you. I might need a few days."

"Take all the time you need. We can handle things here until you're ready to come back."

"I'll be back for the black-tie event."

Her eyes moved to him, and he wanted to pull her into his arms, but he knew she didn't need that right now. She was holding on by a thread and would hate to show her emotions in public.

"Will you manage at the office?"

"Of course. I can get a temp in to cover."

"Will you come with me?"

The question shocked him so much that he didn't respond straight away. But his answer would always be yes if she needed him, and that was a revelation too. He'd never put anyone above work or his own personal wants and desires, but he knew for her he'd drop anything and everything.

"I'm sorry, that was silly."

Nadia stood abruptly and pushed past him before he could react fast enough.

"Nadia, wait."

He almost caught her as the lift closed, her lip wobbling the last thing he saw before the doors blocked her from sight.

"Give her a minute to process."

Gideon rounded on Bás. "What the fuck were you thinking telling her here? You could have given her some privacy before landing her with that news."

"She needed it done in public to help her keep it together. Duchess doesn't like showing her emotions to anyone. I gave her a reason to keep it together in front of me."

Fuck, that made sense but he still didn't like it. "I'm going with her."

"I was counting on it."

"You knew she'd ask?"

"Fuck no, but it works out better for us. We're a little thin on the ground with Snow and Charlie out on maternity leave, Bishop hovering like an overprotective mother hen, and Val avoiding me."

"Why is Val avoiding you?"

"That's a long story, and one I'm not sharing with you."

Gideon waved his hand dismissively. "Fine, I don't care. Just make it so I can go with her."

"I'll handle it on my end, you just need to keep this deal with Macey going and manage your brother."

"I can work from my laptop anywhere. Plus, Damon can handle anything else I need, unless you're keeping him hidden away?"

"No, we think you were the target."

"You know something?"

"No, but we're looking into a few things. Having you out of the way will make things easier. Plus, she needs you."

"I wouldn't be anywhere else."

Bás folded his arms across his chest. "Would've been nice if you said that, dumbass, rather than gaping like a fish with his dick in his hand."

Gideon shook his head. "A fish with a dick? You're not right in the head."

"Ain't that the truth. I think it's all the oestrogen I'm surrounded by these days. My point is, you need to get up there and show her she can count on you. If you don't feel that way about her you need to back the fuck up because if you hurt her, I'll rip your head off and shit down your throat, and believe me, that's only the beginning."

"God, what is with you people and threatening me?"

Bás shrugged. "It's our love language."

"I'd be flattered if I wasn't so worried about Nadia."

Gideon began to walk to the lift so he could fix this and Bás walked beside him, both men stopping for the car to come down.

"Not that it's anyone's business but ours but I care about her. I won't let anyone hurt her if it's in my power to stop it."

Bás slapped him on the shoulder. "Good man. I'll be in touch about getting you a flight to Italy. We want it off the radar if possible. The less people who know where you are the better."

Gideon nodded as he stepped into the elevator and pressed the button for his floor. He spent the minute it took to reach his floor to absorb the news of her mother's death and felt a pang in his chest. He'd been lost when his mother died and, on reflection, wasn't sure he ever got over the loss.

Nadia was nowhere in sight when he exited and scanned the floor, so he headed into his office and stopped when he found her curled up on his couch, her shoulders shaking silently. In all his years he'd never had the urge to protect someone like he wanted to protect Nadia. Which was ironic considering who she was and why she was there in the first place.

Striding to the sofa, he lifted her in his arms and sat, settling her on his lap as she buried her face, hiding from him. He didn't speak but held her close, stroking her back and murmuring nonsensical words to her. "I'm so sorry, Cookie. It's gonna be okay. I'm not gonna leave you to deal with this alone." He kissed her hair, wishing he could absorb her pain into himself.

"I never cry."

"I know."

Her hiccup almost broke him, and he knew without a doubt he was in love with the woman in his arms. What a time to have a revelation like that when she was broken and grieving.

"I'm sorry."

"Hey, you have nothing to be sorry for. When my mum died, I cried for weeks after, and even now sometimes her loss hits me and almost brings me to my knees."

Nadia pulled away, her face red and blotchy, eyes red and swimming with her pain. "Really?"

"Yes. The loss of a parent is hard. Even though as a society we're taught to expect it, we're never truly prepared to lose the person who's our anchor."

"I just feel like I have so many regrets right now. We were never close. She was hardly the effusive motherly type, but I loved her, and she loved me. We were just very different people."

"I think it's natural to have regrets, but you can't live like that, Cookie. You will for a while but eventually, you'll feel less raw and be able to process it all."

Nadia tried to sit up and extract herself from his arms, but he tightened them around her.

"Why do you call me Cookie?"

"Because every time I look at you my mouth waters."

She stroked his face, and he closed his eyes. "You're not who I thought you were."

Gideon placed his hand over hers and turned his lips to her palm. "I am, Nadia. I'm still the arrogant prick you met. You just make me want to be a better man."

"This is crazy."

"I know, but I can't stop the way you make me feel and I don't want to."

"Neither do I."

Her words washed over him, and he had to be cautious that this wasn't a reaction to the news of her mother's death. "Let's take it one day at a time and keep an open mind."

"Okay."

He let her hand go but tightened his arms on her.

"I'm fine now, you can let me go."

"Never." His voice was choked when he said it and he coughed to clear it as she looked at him with wide eyes. He desperately wanted to blurt out how absolutely in love with her he was but now wasn't the time and he didn't have a clue how she felt about him, just that she felt this connection. "I'm coming with you."

Nadia shook her head. "No, it was a silly reflex. I can handle this on my own." Her bottom lip disappeared between her teeth and her eyes welled again.

He cupped her shoulders in his hands, her warm skin silky under his palms. "I know you can handle it, but you don't have to, and I want to be there for you. Please let me be there for you."

"Are you sure? We have so much happening here."

He wanted to smile like an adolescent in the first throws of love at her use of the term 'we'. He wanted to be a 'we' with her. "It's all settled. I'm going to work from my laptop and Damon can handle anything else." She was weakening but he knew he needed to appeal to her sense of responsibility. "Plus, Bás says it would be better if I go with you because it makes life easier with the team being stretched."

"How will you oversee Carter with the Macey deal?"

"I can Skype or Zoom, and Damon can be here in person. He might look soft and squidgy, but Damon is the cleverest business mind in our family, shit, that I know. He just hates it and doesn't have the stomach for all the bullshit."

Her lips tipped and he felt the knot in his belly ease at the sight. She might be hurting right now but she'd be okay, she was strong and resilient and his. She just didn't know that last bit yet.

"Fine, as long as you're sure. I know we need to keep this deal intact now."

"We will."

"I need to head home and pack and sort a flight."

"Bás is handling our flight. We can head to your place and pick up some stuff now."

"What about you?"

He hadn't thought about him since hearing the news, his only thoughts were for her and her comfort. He shrugged. "I can pick something up when we get there."

"You mean you don't have clothes that aren't three-thousand-pound suits?"

He chuckled and kissed her lightly on the mouth. He didn't take it further. It was enough for having her in his arms. Seeing the lightness back in her eyes made his worry for her ease a little. "I'll have you know I own sweatpants, jeans, and even a few pairs of board shorts."

"Wow, you really like to cut loose when you're not cutting people down in the boardroom?"

"I'd like to do very bad things to you in the board room, but for now, let's get going."

He stood and helped her, relieved to see a little more colour in her face.

"I'm gonna need to see those sweatpants on you."

He held her hand as he wandered over to his desk and packed up his laptop and any important documents he might need, including grabbing his passport from the safe in the corner of the room. "Why the sweatpants?"

Her lips turned up at the corners. "I'll explain on the flight."

Gideon shrugged. "Okay, now I'm intrigued."

"Not as much as I am."

He knew she was deflecting away from her mother's death but if that was what she needed, he was happy to give it to her. "I need to call Damon, really quick."

"That's fine, I need to grab my bag and fix my face."

He cupped her chin and tipped her eyes to him. "Your face is as beautiful as ever."

"You have to say that because you want in my pants."

"No, I said it because you are the most breathtakingly beautiful woman I've ever met, and I *am* getting in your pants eventually. I just need to wear you down." He grinned and kissed her again because keeping his hands and mouth off her was almost impossible.

"Sweet talker."

He smacked her ass and let her go and she winked at him. He suspected she might fall apart again when she was alone, but she needed that and he'd give her anything she wanted.

When he was alone, he dialled his brother and waited for him to answer. He knew Lotus would be monitoring the call but that didn't matter to him.

"Hey, Gideon, I just heard. How is she?"

A twinge of jealousy pinched his belly and he had to bite down the irrational feeling. "She's hanging in there, but obviously upset."

"Yeah, I bet. Is there anything I can do?"

"Yes. I'm going to Italy with her. I need you to handle any face-to-face meetings here."

Silence met his announcement and he waited for yet another warning not to hurt Nadia.

"Just be careful. I know you closed yourself off to love but I can also see the chemistry between you two. Her job won't make life easy for the two of you to have a relationship."

"A relationship?" He was stalling and mentally panicking at the thought but then he pictured her face earlier and knew he could do it for her.

"Yes, a relationship. I see the way you look at her and you've never looked at a woman like you do her. When you love, Gideon, you do it with your whole heart. Just be careful."

"You make me sound like a fucking Care Bear."

"You are a big old Care Bear."

"Jerk."

Damon chuckled. "Takes one to know one."

"Asshole."

"Yeah, well, this asshole has your back and I'll handle anything here. Just look after her and give her my love."

Gideon gritted his jaw. "I'll do no such thing."

His brother's deep laugh filled his ear as he hung up. Despite the way the day had turned out, he felt hope crowd his mind. His life was a mess, but he had Nadia, a woman he could see himself having a real future with, and his relationship with Damon was as tight as ever. Before long, Carter and Marsha would be a distant memory and his father would be out of his life for good, too.

A pang of regret filled him at that, and he considered what Nadia was going through and if he'd lament cutting his dad from his life. It was a lot to think about and not something he needed to decide right now.

Nadia walked towards him, her face washed free of the makeup her tears had smeared, and his heart hitched in his chest. She was so beautiful it hurt to look at her for too long. Like looking into the sun and wanting to keep doing so forever but knowing you had to look away or it would be too much.

"Ready?"

Her innocent question hit him, and he wondered if he'd ever be ready for her, but he knew in that second he sure as fuck wasn't ready to walk away. And he probably never would be either.

CHAPTER 13

Duchess pulled the sunglasses over her eyes as she exited the car Bás had sent to bring her and Gideon to RAF Northolt. On the tarmac sat a beautiful sleek Gulfstream, highlighted by the late afternoon sun glinting over the horizon. Hurricane waved and she held up her hand before turning back to Gideon to ask him to grab the bags, but he was already hefting them out of the car.

"Thank you."

His smile made her belly flip and, despite her exhaustion and grief, she felt desire sweep through her for this man. No, more than desire, something less tangible than that, a feeling of belonging she'd never known she was missing until him.

"Duchess." Hurricane's big arms swept her into a hug and she swallowed down the tears as she returned his embrace.

"I'm so sorry."

He looked at her as she blinked rapidly and nodded.

"Thank you."

Hurricane took the bags from Gideon and led the way inside the aircraft, ducking his head at the top.

LETHAL SALVATION

"We'll be in Italy in about two and a half hours. Why don't you get settled while I just finish up my pre-flight checks."

"Wow, she's a beauty." Her eyes scanned the interior of the jet, spotting the leather seating, the dining area, and she knew it would have a private bedroom and bath at the rear. Black piano glass finish along the walnut woodwork gave the final touch of luxury to this aircraft.

"She really is special."

"Who does it belong to?"

"A friend of Jack, from what I understand."

Duchess smiled, Jack, her friend and the man who had given her this team and who had saved her ass more than once. Who knew, in the hells of the sandbox, that such a friendship would thrive and last. He'd already reached out, offering his condolences and letting her know that, if she needed anything, he and Astrid were there for her.

"He's a good guy."

"Should I be jealous?"

Duchess glanced back at Gideon who was grinning at her with a tenderness that made the already fine emotions wobble.

"When you meet him, you'll understand, but no, Jack and I have never been that and his wife is a firecracker who would beat my ass if I even thought it, which luckily I don't."

Hurricane smirked and ducked his head out as he went to finish his checks and she moved to her seat while Gideon stashed their bags, before settling in beside her.

His hand covered hers. "How you holding up?"

"I'm okay. Just a little tired."

His arm came around her as Hurricane closed the doors of the plane.

"I'm not surprised, you must be running on fumes."

"So must you, neither of us have slept properly in days."

His nose wrinkled and he lifted his arm to flex his bicep, the form-fitting t-shirt he wore with jeans showing off the tattoo on his arm.

"Nah, I'm a tough macho man. I don't need sleep."

She shook her head with a smile. "So tough macho men don't need sleep?"

"Of course not, we are men, the hairy hunter."

"You gonna club me over the head and drag me back to your cave?"

"No, I want you wide awake when I carry you back to my cave. But I would suggest we try and get a few hours of sleep while we can."

The plane taxied down the runway and, in minutes, they lifted into the sky as smoothly as silk. Hurricane was one of the best pilots in the world, and the fact that he had been discharged from the military for what amounted to an act of heroism was a travesty. Their loss was Shadow's gain, but she knew he missed flying as much as he had before and was glad he could do this, she just hated the reason why.

"Come on."

Gideon unbuckled her seat belt as they reached cruising altitude and led her toward the back.

She eyed the bed and cocked a brow at him, but her body was already getting on board with this plan.

"Don't look at me like that, my intentions are noble, I'm gonna hold you safe while you sleep."

"Tease." She winked and climbed on the bed, making sure to give him a nice view of her ass in these jeans as she did. A swat on her butt made her yelp before his arms came around her waist. She lay beneath him, his hard body hovering over her as he gazed down at her.

"No teasing, Cookie. I just want to look after you but later, when you're rested, I have every intention of blowing your mind and wiping away every thought in your pretty little head."

"Yeah, how you gonna do that?" Her voice was husky and

aroused and she could feel his cock, hard and wanting against her belly.

His nose skimmed her neck and he sniffed, before placing a kiss behind her ear. "I could tell you, but I'm not going to. You can close those beautiful eyes instead and dream of it, while I hold you."

Duchess wanted to argue, but a giant yawn hit her and she couldn't.

Gideon turned them so she was tucked into him, her back to his front, his arm over her middle, his biceps under her head.

"It's gonna involve sweatpants."

"What is?"

"My dream."

Gideon chuckled as he smoothed her hair back from her face, his lips finding her cheek.

"Whatever you want, Nadia. I have a feeling I would give you just about anything."

Those were the last words she heard before sleep claimed her.

∼

She had to admit the sleep had done her the world of good. Landing in Naples, they took a car Bás had hired for them, and Gideon drove towards the town where her mother had lived and worked most of her life. The fifteen years in the United Kingdom, raising Duchess with her father, the only time she had been away.

"This is a beautiful area."

She glanced across at Gideon, his hands firm on the steering wheel, his forearm muscle shifting as he drove, and her body tingled with the need to feel his hands on her skin; not just his hands but all of him, everywhere.

"Nadia?"

She shook off the thought. "Sorry what?"

"This place, it's beautiful."

"It really is perfect although I sometimes believe it was leaving the place she loved that caused my parents' divorce."

"Yeah?"

Duchess nodded as the scenery sped past them.

"Yes, I drove a wedge into their relationship. Torre del Grecco is where her heart lived, and she always missed it. Did you know it's the biggest producer of coral in Europe and the biggest producer of cameo brooches since the seventeenth century? The locals are even known as Corallini because of it and my mother was one of them. Technically, so am I because I was born here."

"Ha, I didn't know that. It explains the fiery temper though."

"I don't have a fiery temper."

"If you say so, dear."

"As if you'd ever be a yes man."

He glanced across at her. "Is that what you'd want?"

"No, I want you as you are now. Fierce and formidable to the outside world and sweet and squidgy with me."

Gideon laughed and she thought if he could bottle that sound and the feeling it gave her, he'd cure half the world's problems.

"Squidgy? I'm not liking these analogies. First Damon calling me a Care Bear and now you're calling me squidgy."

"Damon is hilarious."

"He is not, he's a pain in my ass."

"You're lucky you have each other."

"I know, I don't know what I would have done without him when we were younger especially."

Silence filled the car and she let her thoughts wander as they drove through the town. It was easy to see why her mother loved it so much, but enough to walk away from her only child she didn't know? She knew her mother hadn't abandoned her but when she turned eighteen and went to university to study languages her mother had taken the opportunity to move back here.

Pulling up to the restaurant her grandparents had owned and

then her mother it was hard to see the lights out and the smells she loved not wafting from the door.

"I loved the smells that came from this place when we would visit when I was young. Garlic, herbs, tomato, the scents of my early years."

"How old were you when you moved to the UK?"

"About three. My father had moved us for his work, and I don't really remember living here."

"Do you speak Italian?"

"Grazie per essere qui e tenermi insieme quando voglio crollare."

Gideon's voice dropped as he turned into her. "What does that mean?"

"It means 'Thank you for being here and holding me together when I want to fall apart'."

His fingers swept her hair from her cheek as his eyes softened with something she didn't want to evaluate right now.

"There is nowhere I would rather be, Nadia."

His lips met hers, and it was easy to sink into the kiss and let him wash away the grief and pain she knew she'd face when she walked inside that building. He pulled away and rested his forehead against her neck.

"You ready."

"No."

"If you need to sit in this car all night, then that's what we'll do, Nadia. Just let me know what you need."

"A time machine."

"Ah baby, if it was in my power to give it to you, I would, but that's the one thing I can't give you."

"I know. Let's just get this over with."

Inside she flicked on the lights as memories assailed her, causing her legs to feel weak. An arm around her waist kept her steady as she slowly walked through the restaurant, then the kitchen where her mother had taught her to make gnocchi and pasta. As her feet carried her up the stairs, she was grateful to have Gideon here. She wasn't sure she could have faced it alone.

The flat above the restaurant was small, with two bedrooms, a small kitchen and a living area with a small balconette where her mother would sit in the evening and crochet as she listened to music or the sounds of the town.

"It's like she just popped out to the shops. Everything is how she would've left it."

A half-finished crossword puzzle, that would remain that way forever, sat on the coffee table. A blanket that needed the edges finishing was in the wool box beside the chair she favoured.

Moving to the mantel above the gas fire, she gazed at the pictures of her through the years. Some with both of them, some including her grandparents and some of her alone. It was seeing those, and the certificates on the walls of all she'd achieved, she realised how much her mother had loved her.

"I can't be here." Her words were choked, and Gideon's arms came around her as he steered her to the door.

"Let's head to the hotel. We can come back when you're ready."

That was the problem though, she didn't think she'd ever be ready.

CHAPTER 14

HE'D FELT THE WAY HER MEMORIES HAD SWAMPED NADIA WHEN SHE entered her mother's home. He didn't know how he'd had such a visceral reaction but it was like his emotions were tied up in hers.

Coming to the hotel had been the right call. He'd run her a bath and left her to relax while he sorted out room service for them both. It was late but she needed food and he needed a minute to get his thoughts under control before he blurted out how stupidly in love with her he was.

Only he'd fall in love with a woman he'd never slept with and hardly knew. Yes, they'd spent time together this last year but he didn't know her enough. But maybe that was part of love, never feeling like you knew enough but also knowing the person inside out and out.

"Hey."

Nadia had put on a cream robe, as she walked toward him towel drying her hair.

"You hungry? I had them send up a few different dishes for us."

"I am actually."

"I figured we could have a carpet picnic. Less formal." He'd laid cushions on the floor and set the food in the centre.

"And you wore the sweatpants too."

Gideon felt the blush stain his cheeks. He'd worn them for her, not really understanding the attraction but wanting to do something to make her smile. "I did."

"So, what do we have?"

"Well, I ordered Pizza Quattro Stagioni, gnocchi with clams, risotto with shrimp, and Pappardelle pasta with mushrooms. I also ordered some tiramisu if you have room after. Oh, and a bottle of chianti to go with it"

"Wow, this looks amazing."

"I'm glad. You need to eat and keep up your energy."

He watched as Duchess dug into the food, enjoying the simple pleasure of being with her and loving that she was enjoying her food.

"You know, my mother taught me to make fresh pasta and gnocchi before I was ten."

"You enjoy cooking?" Gideon asked.

"I do when I have time but that doesn't happen often and it's different with how I live."

"So, do you live with the rest of the team?"

"I do. We have separate apartments within the structure, but we eat together a lot."

"You seem more like family than co-workers."

Duchess licked her lip where some of the mushroom sauce had dribbled, and he felt his dick harden.

"When you put your life in someone's hands on a regular basis, they become family real quick. I never had siblings but each one of my team is my sibling of circumstance and I know they would give their life for mine and I would do the same."

"Wow, that's dedication."

"Not really, it's love. You would do the same for Damon."

Gideon pursed his lips and nodded. "I would. He's my baby brother, and I'll always protect him."

"Same for me with those guys."

"What about kids? Do you see children in your future?"

"I do. I want a family. I feel like I missed out on that closeness with my own."

He could listen to her all night. "How so?" He poured her another glass of the fragrant red wine.

"You trying to get me drunk?"

He stood and reached for her. "Nah, just buzzed."

Her robe gaped and he wanted to trace the pattern of the tattoos on her neck with his tongue.

Nadia stepped closer so her nipples brushed against his chest. "What are you thinking?"

He sucked in air through his nose, trying to calm his hard dick and failing. This woman was like a drug, and he couldn't remember ever wanting someone more. "That I want you, but I should wait."

Her fingers ran down his bare chest and he gulped as his dick strained, wanting to feel her tight pussy contracting around him.

"What if I don't want to wait?" She looked down at the tent in his pants. "And these sweatpants sure tell a story of a man who doesn't want to wait."

"Yeah, it's kind of hard to hide in these."

Her breath feathered his pecs and his belly tightened as her fingers toyed with the edge of the waistband. Just an inch and she'd be touching him. He was almost dying with need for her.

"Now you see why I like them."

His lips nuzzled her cheek as he teased her like she was him. His hand reached out to take the glass from her and place it on the side table. "If you want it, take it, Nadia."

He wasn't sure what he was expecting but it sure as hell wasn't her dropping to her knees as she drew his joggers down his thighs, letting his cock bounce free.

As she took hold of him in her hand and stroked his eager dick, her eyes finding his, he groaned. "Fuuuck."

If he could live in this moment until the day he died, he'd be a happy man, but he was greedy. His thumb rubbed along her bottom lip, tugging the delicate skin down. "Open your mouth for me, Cookie." He kept his eyes on her as she did as he asked. Cupping the hand that held him, he guided his cock to her wet lips. "Suck me."

Her eyes fluttered closed as the electricity in the room seemed to fizz with energy and passion.

"Eyes on me."

Her lids lifted as she took him in her mouth and slowly bobbed her head, laving him in her warm wet heat.

"You're so beautiful taking my cock."

His words seemed to drive her own need and he watched as she loosened her robe with her free hand until it fell open, revealing her perfect body to him. Creamy skin covered her delicious curves. Dark dusky nipples that peaked as he reached out to thrum them with his fingers.

His dick hit the back of her throat and he cupped the back of her head, holding her still, immobile, and her gorgeous hazel green eyes watered but she didn't struggle or fight him. She gave him her trust and he treasured it. Releasing her, he watched her work him, pleasure so hot and intense he wondered how the room wasn't burning around them.

When he thought he couldn't take any more without spilling his seed into her gorgeous mouth, he leaned forward and hooked her under her arms. Lifting her, he walked toward the bedroom as her legs wrapped around him.

Dipping his head, he kissed her deep and long, his tongue tasting her and himself, and it only added to the eroticism of the moment. Nadia didn't just let him kiss her, she kissed him back, almost fighting for control and it was like being claimed at the same time as he claimed her.

Dropping her on the bed, he stepped to his bag and drew out a couple of condoms before dropping them on the bed. "I love looking at you."

She was splayed out on the bed like every fantasy he'd had since the day they'd met. Her dark satin-soft hair tumbled about her, her body languid and exposed as she ran her hand over her breast, teasing him.

"I love you looking at me."

"Show me that pussy, Nadia. Spread those gorgeous legs for me and let me see you."

Her legs fell open, revealing the sweetest cunt he'd ever gazed upon. Wet and pink, with no hair to hide her from him. The tattoo from her thigh weaved its way up like a vine skimming her pussy lips and ending on her hip. It made him want to find the man who'd inked her and kill him for having touched what he now considered his.

Bending, he traced the lines from her knee up over the outline and she squirmed, trying to force him to touch her where she needed it most.

"Touch your nipples."

Her hands lifted immediately, and she teased her nipples with her fingers, pinching and pulling as her back arched off the bed.

"Fucking beautiful."

His cock was leaking with the need to be inside her. He thought he could come without a single touch just from watching her like this.

"Touch me."

He smirked, shaking his head. "Tut tut tut, Nadia. You don't give the orders in here. This is my playground and I make the rules."

Her groan was part frustration and part lust as he saw her pussy glisten with her response to his words. "You like that, don't you? Me telling you who's in charge."

His thumb parted her pussy lips and a moan escaped her throat as he pulled back the hood on her clit and rolled it under his thumb with just the slightest pressure.

"Oh God, that's so good."

His lips twitched at her words and he knelt on the bed so he could dip his head. His tongue flicked out and he licked her from the sweet entrance to her pussy to her clit, which pulsed under his tongue.

"Do you want to come, Nadia?"

"Yes." The words seemed to come from deep in her chest, breathy and seductive and he had to wrap his hand around his cock and squeeze to stop himself from spilling all over her belly. Gideon pushed a finger inside her, moaning at the tightness of her pussy before he added a second, fucking her slowly with his hand as his thumb tortured her clit. Her body tightened, her legs shaking as she moaned and whimpered, and then she stilled before her pussy clamped tight around him and her clit pulsed hard against his thumb.

Her cries filled the room and he wanted the whole hotel, fuck no, the whole world, to know this amazing creature was his.

He gentled his hand and slipped his fingers from her, tasting her delicious climax as he sucked her from his fingers. She watched, languid and relaxed, as he stood and slid a condom down his rock-hard cock. Her arousal was written openly over her face. She was real and honest and open with her need for him.

Moving over her, he braced on his elbows on either side of her head, his body covering hers and kissed her deeply. He poured every emotion he was feeling into it and felt her giving him a piece of herself.

His cock nudged her entrance, and he closed his eyes, burying his head in her neck as he pushed inside. Her body was like a glove and fit him like she was made for him. "You're perfect."

He kissed her as he began to move, finding his pleasure in her and giving back just as she was. They were so in sync it was as if they had been lovers for a lifetime. Moving and touching like they knew every hidden pleasure point and yet it was all new and exciting.

Pulling back, he sat on his heels as he grasped her hips and pulled her up at an angle. Nadia cried out as his cock hit a new place inside her and her walls fluttered around him. Sweat dripped down his chest as he stroked inside her, an inferno building inside him at the rightness of this moment and this woman.

He was on the tip of spilling his feelings for her but knew now wasn't the time. Pulling out, he flipped her to her belly and hauled her hips up before thrusting back inside her warm wet pussy. His hand gripped her hip as the other skimmed up her spine, cataloguing the dips and patterns on her skin as they both chased their climax.

"Touch your clit."

Her hand disappeared beneath her and he held her from falling as she tightened around him, screaming his name and flooding his cock with her arousal and climax. She squeezed him so tight he thought he might black out from pleasure but he held on, fucking her through her orgasm before he let go and fucked her with a primal need snapping at his heels.

As he spilled his come inside her, he hated the barrier that kept them from feeling it all. It was that moment that made it clear just how gone for her he was because, far from having a baby with her scaring him, he wanted it. To make a life with her, to have her body change as she carried his child.

Her body gave and he sagged against her back, kissing the ridges of her spine before cupping her chin, and turning her for his kiss. He took her mouth in a languid kiss before releasing her.

Escaping to the bathroom, he took care of the condom and washed his hands before wetting a cloth with warm water and heading back to the bedroom. There he found the woman he was madly in love with fast asleep, her body finally giving in to the grief and exhaustion. Quickly and gently, he cleaned her up before throwing the washcloth on the side. Climbing into bed, he brought her into his arms and tugged the quilt around them. Kissing her head, he allowed the thoughts he'd bit back to be free.

"I love you, Nadia. You're mine now and I'll find a way to prove you can trust that I'll never walk away from you."

He stayed awake for hours thinking of her and the situation they were in because of his family. He knew he'd do whatever it took to keep this woman and make her see how much he cared.

CHAPTER 15

As the wheels touched down on the tarmac of RAF Northolt, Duchess had mixed feelings. She was glad to be home with her people, her family, and yet already she missed the time she'd got to spend with Gideon. Just the two of them, sharing stories of their lives or tidbits of inconsequential information that would seem mundane to others, but each sentence revealed another layer to the man she had to acknowledge she had feelings for.

He'd held her hand as she stood at the graveside surrounded by her mother's friends. Held her up when her grief seemed too heavy and made her forget the guilt and confusion over her loss.

Up until now, sex had been a release for her, a way to let off steam and she'd had good sex, but she'd never felt what Gideon made her feel. As if they were connected on a level she couldn't explain. He was tender, dominant, demanding and he always seemed to know what she needed before even she did, and he gave it freely. His pleasure was so caught up in hers that it was like a dance, a dangerous erotic tango filled with passion, and she had to admit a few times she'd almost blurted out words she'd never said to another.

"Hey, you okay?"

She turned as Gideon got the bags from the overhead locker and offered him a reassuring smile. "Yes. Just eager to get back to work." She saw doubt ease across his handsome features and reached out to touch the worry on his brow, smoothing the skin away. "You'll get wrinkles."

His lips twisted into a smirk. "You saying I look old?"

He hooked her around the waist and hauled her close, palming her ass cheek with his free hand as he kissed her as if it was his sole purpose in life. She let him sweep her away, the desire and need for him a constant thrum in her veins. When he lifted his head, he was as affected as she, his eyes swirling with promise.

"Um, I'm gonna need more of that later."

A throat clearing beside her startled her and she went to move, but Gideon held her fast and she settled as she spied Bás. Gideon clearly wanted to make a statement and she wasn't sure she did, but she wouldn't fuss. This meant more to him than it did her and so what if she and Gideon were together, it wasn't like it was a first for the team.

"Bás, what are doing here?"

"I wanted to give you both an update."

Bás clocked the intimacy between them but said nothing and didn't react, and she relaxed a little. "Well let's get to it then."

Hurricane would find his own way back after he'd finished with his post-flight checks. He'd admitted to her on the return flight, when she'd sat with him while Gideon read through some work documents, that he missed flying. She hated that he'd been denied his passion when he was so good at it. She wondered if there was a way to give him some of that back and an idea formed. She'd need to speak to Bás about it first, but it worked with their cover and helped Hurricane.

She sat in the back with Gideon and Bás in the passenger seat as Titan drove.

"Let me have it."

Bás smirked. "Workaholic much?"

"Um, pot meet kettle."

Gideon chuckled at them and she winked at him. "You'll get used to us, don't worry."

"Oh, I'm not worried. If it's one thing Carter has done, it's broadened my horizons by inviting you and your team into my life."

"Well shit, that sounds like you might actually like us, Gideon." Titan looked at them in the rear-view mirror.

"Let's just say you're growing on me."

"Like groinal fungus, baby."

"Gross."

"Now we've whittled this elite team down to a sexually transmitted disease, can we move on, please?"

"Sure, what you got?"

"Well, we've moved to the London safe house for starters. Our intel leads us to understand that Marsha was behind the attack on you, Gideon. We've managed to find footage of the man we believe was shooting at you. Unfortunately, he was found face down in the Thames two days ago."

"Anyone we know?"

"Nobody who's been on our radar. Richard Brown. He was a British national, ex-army, dishonourable discharge for conduct unbecoming. He became a gun for hire. He was responsible for a few low-level hits but nothing like this."

"How do we know it was Marsha and not my brother?"

"Carter has his own team, and he might have been bragging but he wasn't wrong. His team wouldn't have missed. They're all elite former special forces soldiers and, in another life, I would've hired half of them for this team."

"Why hasn't Marsha got the same kind of protection if she's involved like we think she is?"

"Her protection is provided by Project Cradle and we think she went outside for this because it wasn't part of the plan."

"So, it isn't happy families after all?"

"No."

They stopped at a Victorian-style warehouse in Cottonfields that the team owned. It looked rundown from the outside but had been converted inside. The doors opened and Titan drove straight inside the bottom level, which had been utilised as a garage and storage area.

She moved to get out and saw Gideon looking at her, his skin pale as he looked around.

"Are you okay?"

He cocked his head looking at her intently. "Where are we?"

"Our safe house in London."

"You didn't drug me, does that mean…"

He didn't finish his sentence and she immediately saw the concern and read the reason. "It means Bás is trusting you." She reached for his hand. "And believe me when I say that doesn't come lightly."

He let out a breath like the air going out of a balloon. "Great."

"You honestly didn't think I'd let anyone hurt you, did you?" She was surprisingly hurt by that thought.

"I don't know what I thought, but after last time, it crossed my mind that I might end up with cement boots."

Duchess laughed. "Don't be silly. Nobody does that anymore."

Gideon pretended fear and she laughed, and he joined in with a grin. "Oh, that was nasty."

"Serves you right for thinking the worst of me."

"Yeah, I guess I deserved that. I just… I've never known anyone like you and it's unsettling."

"I know but we're gonna fix that."

She led the way upstairs to the open-plan layout where the rest of the team was waiting around the giant dining table. A huge pot of chilli filled the room with a gorgeous smell that made her belly rumble loudly.

"I guess by the sound of Duchess' gut we're gonna eat and talk at the same time." Lotus came over and hugged her in a rare sign of affection. "Hey, how are you doing?"

"I'm okay. Processing bit by bit."

"It takes time. Just let it come and don't be shocked if it hits you out of the blue sometimes."

"Thanks, Naz," she said using her friend's real name.

"Now dig in. I don't cook often so enjoy." She pointed a spoon at Gideon. "Hope you like it hot."

"I can handle it."

Duchess smirked. "Leave him alone, Lotus."

"Hmm, sticking up for the boy toy, must be serious. Hope that shit isn't catching."

Her eyes moved to Damon who was sitting across the other side of the room and watching Lotus as if he was trying and failing to figure her out. She hoped that wasn't going to become a thing. Lotus would chew him up and spit him out and she didn't want that for Damon. He was a good guy and Lotus had enough baggage to sink the Titanic and no intention of facing any of it.

"Enough. We have shit to talk about and it's not you, Lotus."

Bás sat at the head of the table, and she motioned for Gideon to take a seat beside her and Reaper.

"Burn." Reaper chuckled and ducked as Lotus threw a pot of chilli flakes at him.

"As I was saying, we think Marsha and Carter are at odds. We believe that Carter is using the Macey deal as a way out from under his mother's thumb."

"Wait, you think Carter is blackmailing his own mother?"

"Not just her but essentially, yes."

"Where does my father sit in all this?"

"Where he's always been, a pawn in a game he doesn't know the rules to. He isn't involved with this, but he's up to his eyeballs in gambling debts and Carter is using it to his advantage."

Duchess took a spoonful of the delicious chilli as she mulled over her thoughts and what all this could mean. It was the one dish Lotus excelled at and she wouldn't give the recipe to anyone. "Where does Hansen sit in all this?"

Duchess watched Bás' expression go hard, a flicker of his jaw his only tell before he rolled his neck.

"Hansen knows Marsha from way back. When she entered the original Project Cradle, he wasn't around but he came on a few years later. After it was allegedly disbanded, they kept in touch."

"Were they lovers?"

"Hansen likes to manipulate the women in his life with sex, so most likely they were or still are."

"So is it likely Hansen is on her side and providing help?"

"Hansen is always on Hansen's side, so no, we don't think so. Watchdog found a draft email from Carter's personal account stating he wanted out of Project Cradle and just wanted to handle the trafficking side of it. He doesn't like the heat he's getting and thinks it's not giving them the financial return it warrants."

"It won't be to him. Project Cradle is a long game, and only really benefits people in power who want to appear squeaky clean."

"That was a rookie error leaving it there for us to find."

"Exactly, which is why we think it was a test to see who was looking."

"But won't that mean Hansen will have seen it?"

"Yes, which means there's a power struggle happening."

"That we can exploit?"

Bás pointed his fork at her. "Exactly."

"We need to speak to Carter again and see if we can find a way to make him tell us."

"He promised me he'd look into who shot me and tell me at the black-tie tomorrow."

Duchess glanced at Gideon who had been relatively quiet until now. "You think he will?"

Gideon looked at Damon who shrugged. "I don't know, but he'd seemed different, more cooperative."

"Because he wants something," Gideon spat.

"Yes, but even so, the fact he wants something from us could still work to our advantage. We should divide and conquer. Lotus and Damon can keep Marsha busy while we try and talk to Carter."

Lotus gave Damon a grin before draping herself over his shoulder. "What do you say, lover, can we pull it off?"

Damon rolled his eyes. "I can handle it if you can. But you've got to promise not to fall in love with me."

"Ha, as if."

Lotus moved away and Duchess got the distinct feeling she was missing something with those two.

"That's settled then. We'll keep the plan the same, but you guys know what to do."

"Do we have an update on Hansen's whereabouts?"

"Germany was the last sighting."

"We really need to pin this fucker down," Reaper growled.

"Agreed. This has gone on long enough."

"Something tells me this is coming to a head."

Something about the way Bás said it made Duchess shiver. The time was coming for her to have a chat with her boss and find out just what he was hiding from her and the team regarding Hansen.

"Well looks like it's time to go dress shopping."

Lotus grabbed her hand and pulled her towards the stairs that led to an upper floor where an array of provisions was stored, including clothing, props, disguises, weapons, and spare comms.

Duchess groaned and glanced at Gideon, who'd rushed to catch up. She wanted to be with him, to go back to the little bubble they'd created in Italy but real life was pulling them apart already. He pulled her from Lotus gently with a wink and gave her a grin that made her body go up in flames. The things that look conveyed should be illegal.

"I'm going to catch up with Damon, but I'll see you later."

His head descended and he kissed her, his hand cupping the back of her head and moving her exactly where he wanted her. If he hadn't stopped when he did, she was sure her legs would have buckled.

"Jesus, that was hot. I need to go call Lucía." Reaper jogged past them and Gideon smiled.

"Your friends are weird."

Duchess laughed. "Yeah, I guess they are."

CHAPTER 16

Gideon waited at the bottom of the steps in the main room of the warehouse they were calling home for now and paced. The last twenty-four hours had been crazy. From arriving here, to the discussion about Carter, to the chilli that despite burning away his tastebuds had been delicious, and not, as he'd suspected, poisonous.

"Stop pacing, Gideon. This isn't fucking prom."

"We didn't have a prom, dickhead."

Damon shook his head at his remark and leaned against the wall where they were waiting for Nadia and Lotus to meet them for the damn party.

He hated parties and this one was shaping up to be the worst in history. He had to walk into the viper's pit with a woman he cared about knowing that at least one person in the room wanted him dead and had tried to kill him.

Worse was the realisation that if another attempt was made, she'd try and defend him again. He'd tried to talk to Bás about it but the man shut him down, telling him that Duchess was too good at her job for him to undermine her. He grudgingly respected the man for it, but it didn't help his nerves.

A noise at the top of the stairs had him glancing up with a gasp. His chest contracted and for a second, he couldn't draw enough air into his lungs, his heart seemed to swell taking up all the space. He knew if he died now he'd never get the chance to tell her how stupidly in love with her he was. "Wow."

He took her hand as she reached the bottom step and the world around them fell away. Her dress was dark green with a heavily beaded square neckline and no sleeves. The skirt was full, in satin material the same shade as the beading and fell to the floor. Her hair had been pulled away from her face and her make-up was smoky and sultry and screamed sex. Her tattoos only enhanced the overall effect, elevating her to a level that was, in his humble opinion, unparalleled. If he were in any way inclined, he'd spout poetry about her beauty but he was not.

"You like it?"

"Like it? I have no words to describe how stunning you are."

"It has pockets."

Nadia put her hands in the pockets of the skirt and wiggled her shoulders. He couldn't help but return her joyful smile and although this wasn't a date or a real party, this feeling inside him was. "In all my days on this earth, I've never seen anything as beautiful both inside and out as you right at this moment."

"Gideon, if you make me cry, I won't be happy."

He settled his hands on her hips and drew her close, kissing her temple. "I'm sorry, Cookie. Forgive me?"

"I forgive you, but only if you make it up to me later." Her breath was warm as she turned her head into his neck and kissed his jaw with a shiver.

"Oh, baby, I have so many plans for you later."

"Are we ready to go?"

Gideon lifted his head to see Lotus waiting with Damon, who looked as star-struck as he probably did right now. Only his eyes were on Lotus, who was wearing a navy blue dress in satin with a one-shoulder décor on her fitted gown that had a slash to the thigh.

She was beautiful but nothing compared to Nadia. She shone like a diamond, a warrior queen with a regal air and proud tilt of her chin that left others in her wake. "Yes, let's go."

Nadia took his arm as he escorted her to the car. As they got inside the limo that Hurricane was driving, he wished they were travelling alone so he could show her everything he couldn't seem to convey with words.

As his parents' home came into view, his stomach tightened in knots and he could sense the same tension from his brother. This place had been the nucleus of so much of his childhood pain, and the happy memories were buried so deep he wasn't even sure they existed anymore.

Hurricane got out, dressed in the formal clothing of a driver, and opened the door for him. Gideon nodded his thanks and turned to offer Nadia his hand. She took it and he wondered how this would feel if it were real. If she was his and they were attending a normal function like this one without the artifice.

They waited, her arm looped through his as Damon helped Lotus out of the car before heading inside. Hurricane would be close in case he was needed, and Reaper, Bás, and Titan were already on the grounds, not that they'd be visible.

The house was large and ostentatious, with opulence and wealth dripping from every gleaming chandelier. Family photos of his father and Marsha with Carter were dotted about but it was as if he and Damon had never existed, wiped from history along with the mother who'd borne them.

"Well, if this isn't a who's who of the wealthiest and most crooked people on the planet then I don't know what is."

Nadia was right. Even he could see that, and he wasn't as versed in the criminal underbelly as she was. Slap bang in the middle of it was Marsha and his father, holding court like the king and queen they believed themselves to be. Marsha spotted them and he saw her eyes go cold, as much as possible with the amount of Botox in her face. His father, however, gave them a smile of welcome.

"Here we go." Gideon led the way as Damon and Lotus followed.

"Gideon, my boy, your mother and I are so glad you could make it."

He could practically hear Marsha's silent outrage and denial. "Dad, Marsha." He greeted his father with a handshake but made no move to kiss Marsha on the cheek as was expected in these fake situations, where everyone pretended to like each other while sharpening the knife that would go in their backs. "I'd like you to meet, Nadia, my girlfriend."

His father kissed Nadia's cheek and he watched Marsha as she sized the woman beside him up and found her wanting as her nose tilted up.

"A delight, my dear."

Marsha sipped her champagne, her beady eyes assessing them. "I haven't heard Gideon mention you before."

"Why would you? From what I understand, you aren't close."

Marsha sniffed. "This one has claws, Gideon. Are you sure you want to stoop to that level? Her body is mutilated too."

"Mutilated?" Nadia repeated.

He felt Nadia squeeze his arm to bring his anger back under control, but it bit and snarled beneath his skin. His instinct was to defend the woman he loved from this demon queen.

"Yes, the marking on your skin. Really, dear, they're very common and vulgar."

Nadia chuckled as his father looked uncomfortable but as ever, he didn't try and curb his wife in any way, just stood there spineless.

"Ah, yes, I see. Well, I don't expect it's something a woman of your generation would understand. It's more of a modern, younger person's thing. Women over sixty don't tend to get it. Much like my generation don't understand the need to fill our bodies with silicone and Botox."

"Sixty! How dare you? I'm barely ten years older than Gideon."

Sadly, that was true. She'd dug her claws into his father with her youth and beauty.

Nadia patted her arm and she flinched. "Of course you are." Her wink sealed the implied insult that she was lying.

Before Marsha could explode, he pulled Nadia away. "Come, darling, let's get a drink."

He left Damon and Lotus to take up the slack, his brother having more tact. Although he wasn't sure Lotus would win any personality competitions. At the bar, he ordered a scotch and white wine for Nadia.

"If this room wasn't full of complete assholes, I'd get down on my knees and beg you to marry me after that little performance."

Nadia laughed. "That was fun. Women like her are a ten a penny in my world and she may think she's meaner than a wet cat, but she isn't anything special. Also, I prefer rubies, not diamonds."

Gideon tucked that piece of information away, hoping one day he'd get a chance to use it, and not feeling any of the panic he'd normally have at the thought of marriage and a lifelong commitment. "Good to know."

"Now, while Damon and Lotus have your parents occupied, why don't you go and speak with Carter over there and I'll slip away and plant these bugs?"

"I don't like the idea of letting you out of my sight in this room with all these disgusting people." The rooms were packed with people he knew and, as some tried to catch his eye and others tried to hide their surprise at him and Damon attending, all he wanted to do was run and get far away.

Nadia slipped her arms under his tux jacket and around his waist as she looked up at him. "I know this is hard for you but this is my job and I'm damn good at it."

"I know that. I've seen it first-hand, but it doesn't make me want to protect you any less. I lo…. You mean a lot to me and I don't want to see you hurt. I'd never forgive myself." He'd been so close to telling her he loved her, he'd worked so hard not to say it in Italy because the time was wrong, and he almost blew it here in front of these people with her friends listening to every word they said.

Nadia rolled her lips as if she was trying to come to a decision before she went up on her tiptoes and spoke quietly into his ear. To the outside world, it looked like she was kissing him and he held her close, his dick already perking up at having her so close. He wasn't sure there'd ever be a time when he wasn't half erect around her. The chemistry was too strong to be contained or dulled.

"I love you, too."

He stilled, sure his brain was playing tricks on him before he turned to look at the woman who'd just rocked his world.

"I wasn't asleep."

As she kissed his cheek and pulled away, he let her, too stunned to respond fast enough. He watched her weave through the other guests until she was lost to his gaze. He felt eyes on him and looked toward Damon who was smirking and lifting his glass, clearly having heard every word. A smile spread over his face that couldn't be contained, something inside him feeling like it might burst with pride and happiness. He moved to go find her and kiss her until she was jelly in his arms, but he was stopped by Carter.

"Gideon, I need to speak with you."

"Can it wait?" He looked past his brother for the woman who completed him and that was the exact feeling she gave him. Completeness.

"No. It's important."

"Fine, what can I do for you?"

"Not here. Let's talk in the library."

"Fine, lead the way."

"No, you go first. I'll follow in a few minutes."

Gideon sighed but knew this was the goal and he should use the opportunity to help end this nightmare. "Fine." Gideon downed the scotch, slammed the glass down and walked away.

The section of the house where the library was housed was quiet and shut off from the rest of the party. Men and women were strategically situated around the house and he lifted his chin to one as he walked past. Nobody tried to bar his entry and he assumed it was because they knew he was one of the family members.

The library was where he felt his mother the most. Her last good days were spent there reading to him and Damon and playing scrabble or chess. It was the one room untouched by Marsha and for that he was grateful.

A few minutes after he arrived, he heard the door behind him open and glanced back to see Carter closing the door on them. He could see the sweat on his brother's brow and the unusual nervousness emanating from him.

"So, what did you want to talk about?"

Carter loosened his tie and looked about the room as if he expected someone to jump out at him.

"Carter."

"Mother ordered the hit on you."

Gideon knew that but having it confirmed was still a difficult pill to swallow, although not surprising. "How do you know?"

"She told me. We argued about it. She thinks you're working with the government to frame us."

"Frame you for what?"

"Oh, come on, Gideon, you know or at least suspect the pies we have our fingers in and none of it's legal."

"Perhaps, but that's a big jump from me being a spy for the government."

"That's what I told her."

"What were you arguing over?"

"We're involved with something called Project Cradle. I was poised to be the next leader of the group but someone mother knows doesn't want to let go of the reins. I told her if I can't run it, I want out."

"Bet she took that well."

Carter smirked "She didn't."

"So who's running things?"

Carter lost his smile and once again began searching the room, the tension licking off his skin. "I can't tell you. But I will say this, it has to do with the Macey deal."

"How so?"

"I have a sister."

Gideon pretended to be shocked. "What?"

"She's a few years older than me and Tarquin Green is her father."

"I don't get it."

"Let's just say there's a lot you don't know about my mother."

"Clearly." Gideon had to try to not look bothered by the information. "How does this involve me, though? What do you need from me?"

"I want your help. I'm going to flip on the project members, and I want your help to do it."

"Flip?"

"I have evidence and unless I get what I'm asking for, I'm going to the police and I'm going to ask for immunity and protection."

"You're going to send your own mother to jail?"

"I have no choice. This is them or me now."

Gideon ran a hand through his hair and turned to school his expression.

"Keep him talking, Gideon."

He almost startled hearing Watchdog in his ear. "What evidence do you have?"

"I can't tell you that."

"Then how the fuck am I meant to help you?"

"I'm going to tell you where the evidence is and you can take it to someone. I know you have help and I know for fact that woman out there is not your fucking girlfriend, so quit bullshitting me."

"Nadia is exactly that."

"No, she isn't so don't lie. You're not the only one with contacts, Gideon, and we both know Nadia Benassi is former MI6."

Gideon lost it, shoving his brother up against the back of the door, his hands tight around his collar. "Is that a fucking threat?"

"Get out of there, Gideon."

The blood was pounding in his ears, his vision tunnelling red as things seemed to unravel around him.

"No threat, brother."

"Who the fuck else knows?"

"Just me."

"How can I trust you?"

"Because I need you to get me out of this. You and Damon."

"Why now? This could be a fucking setup. You already tried setting me up with the casino and a paper trail leading back to me."

"That was mother's idea."

He wanted to deny it but he saw the truth in Carter's eyes. "If you want my help, give me the information first."

"No can do. It's the only thing keeping me alive."

"I thought you had protection?"

"I do, but I can't trust anyone except you and Damon."

Gideon snorted and pushed his brother away, letting him straighten his shirt and smooth his hair. "Why would you trust me? You hate me and the feeling is mutual. You've been the bane of my life and stolen everything from me."

"You and Damon never even gave me a chance."

"Bullshit, we adored you but as you got older, you became more and more of a spoiled brat. Acting like you were the second fucking coming. That you were entitled to everything."

Carter sighed and Gideon saw a different man from the one he'd hated for so long it was a habit now.

"I know, but do you know how hard it is to be the odd one out? I never understood the conversations you and Damon had or the jokes and closeness you shared."

"You were ten years younger, Carter. There was always going to be things you didn't get."

"You made me feel like an outsider."

He absorbed that and tried to examine his own behaviour and

see it from the other side. He hadn't meant to, but perhaps he'd contributed to the ill feeling in his home.

"And to answer the second question, I trust you because deep down you're a good man and I know that despite everything I've done, you wouldn't turn your back on me and let me die."

"You deserve to go to prison for the rest of your life for what you've done, Carter. Those women. How could you do that?"

"I'm not perfect."

"No shit."

"Will you help me?"

"I need to think about it. Come to my office on Monday."

Carter swept a hand through his hair, the cool, controlled adversary gone replaced by a man who was losing control and reaching for a lifeline whether he deserved it or not. Could he be that lifeline? He didn't know but what he did know was that he needed to speak to Nadia and he needed to see her.

"I have to go."

"Okay."

He reached for the door and Carter stopped him with a touch on his arm, the tug on his sleeve so similar to how he'd tug on his trousers as he followed him around as a child.

"Giddy?"

The childhood nickname was one he hadn't heard in years and all because Carter hadn't been able to say Gideon. He closed his eyes a mountain of regret tumbling down on him. "Yes?"

"Be careful. Hansen is onto you, and he has a real hard-on for your team."

Gideon didn't confirm or deny his involvement or ask questions. He could ask that on Monday when he had Nadia with him to soothe the ragged edges of his frayed soul. "I'll see you Monday."

He left the room, taking a deep breath to ease the tightness in his chest. He had the overwhelming urge to run through the rooms, everything having changed in the last ten minutes.

"Relax, Gideon. Duchess just checked in a minute ago. Head towards the main room and she'll be with you shortly."

He'd thought having someone hearing him would be unsettling, but he found it strangely reassuring. He wouldn't be completely happy until she was in his arms again, though. She'd become his true north, his guiding light, and he wondered how he'd ever gotten through life without her.

CHAPTER 17

THE LAST BUG PLANTED IN THE MAIN BEDROOM, DUCHESS BACKED OUT slowly, closing the door with a click. This property was huge and she knew without Gideon, his step-witch, and pathetic excuse for a father, wouldn't be living in such luxury.

A bang made her stop as she walked past one of the other bedroom doors. Another sound like a clank of something falling to the floor made her push the door open and investigate. With so many unknowns on this job, it paid to be careful.

What she found was something she wouldn't have expected in a hundred years.

"Lotus!"

Her friend was pressed up against the wall, her dress askew with Damon scrambling up from his knees. Her eyes found his and he looked away, his cheeks pink as he stepped to cover the woman he'd been pleasuring.

"Jesus Christ, fix your fucking dress."

Lotus looked horrified as Duchess backed out, trying to hide her grin. As her boss, Lotus would get her ass kicked for this breach. She was here working and anyone could have walked in and found them and she would've been vulnerable as hell. Duchess shuddered to think about it as she bounced down the steps and saw Gideon, a panicked look on his face heading towards her.

Her heart soared at the sight of him, such a change in a few short weeks. Uncovering the man behind the suit had led to feelings she'd never expected. Lust, desire yes, but this bone-deep need to walk through fire just to see him smile proved her heart was in way over its head.

"Hey."

He took her in his arms and held her close and she could hear his heart hammering a fast pace beneath her ear. "Is everything okay?" She stroked his broad shoulders as she assessed his face for a visual cue.

"Let's dance and I'll tell you."

He towed her toward the main room and took her in his arms, dragging her close. Her dress didn't allow the kind of contact she wanted but it did hide the arsenal of weapons she had there. "What's up?"

He cocked his head, already looking calmer than when she'd found him. "What makes you think something is up?"

"I can just tell." Duchess didn't elaborate but let him move her around the dance floor.

"I've never known anyone who could read me like you do. It's like my mind is an open book and you just skip to the page you want to read."

She felt the same. He always seemed to know what she needed before she did and gave it freely. How she'd misjudged him at the start made a lie of his words. "Not sure that's true but I know you're stalling right now."

He sighed and dipped his lips to her neck, a shiver passed over her skin as his warm breath hit her pulse. "Carter asked for my help. He wants to go to the police and he knows I'm working with someone and what your former profession was."

Duchess carried on dancing but her desire had fled, replaced by one-hundred percent focus. Her eyes scanned behind her watching for any sign of an attack, but she knew her team had eyes on her and Lotus.

"Does Bás know?"

"Yes, I do know so enough with the lovey-dovey shit."

Duchess smirked at her boss's response in her ear. "We should probably go."

"Agreed."

Gideon stood still as the music faded and a scream that sent chills down her spine rent the air. The room seemed to still, some people realising what the sound was and others so involved in themselves that they didn't notice. She glanced at Gideon, then across at Lotus and Damon, who'd joined the dance floor shortly after them.

Picking up her skirt she ran towards the sound, Gideon on her heels. A crowd had started to gather outside the library doors and she shoved her way through to see Marsha on her knees, her make-up smeared as she sobbed over the dead body of her son.

Gideon braced his hands on her hips as he drew up to her back with a shocked gasp. Reaching for him, she squeezed his hand but made no move to get closer to the scene. There was no helping Carter. A bullet between the eyes wasn't something you recovered from and the wide stare of his unseeing eyes confirmed it.

"Fuck!"

"Help him, someone help him." Marsha cried over and over as she bent over her son, Gideon's father looking pale as he stared in horror.

"Lotus, get these people back." Duchess took control even though they really need to get out of there before the authorities arrived and things got very sticky for the team.

Lotus began ushering people out with her own special brand of persuasion, the room emptying of onlookers. Sirens sang in the distance, and she stepped away from the scene in front of her and pulled Damon and Gideon to one side. "We can't be here, but we can't leave either. This is a crime scene now and with so many witnesses, we can't just disappear."

"What should we do?"

"Damon, go pour your father a drink. He looks like he's about to pass out. Gideon, go with him and see if he can get Marsha to leave too. She's contaminating all the evidence and I need to take a look in private before we have officers all over the place."

"I can do that."

Gideon looked shaken but he cupped her face. "Be careful."

She lifted up on tiptoes and gave him a short, brief kiss to reassure him and herself that things weren't about to go to shit when she knew that was exactly what was happening.

Gideon guided his father by the arm as Damon helped Marsha stand, reminding her that it was a crime scene now and offering to get her a drink.

Lotus joined her as she glanced at the body of the man who'd done so much damage to those she cared about. Was it right he died this way? No. Was it just? She thought perhaps it was. Live by the sword, die by the sword.

"Watch my back, I need to check something."

Lotus nodded as Duchess slipped inside the library and looked at the scene with a clinical eye. The room was clean, not a cushion out of place, so a struggle hadn't taken place there. Crouching down, she examined the wound that had ended Carter's life and noticed it was a nine millimetre. Most likely a Glock 17, like the UK Military used and easy to come by if you knew where to look.

Unlike in the US, handguns weren't owned by every person over eighteen but that didn't mean it would be easy to trace this weapon unless there was something already in the system. She wouldn't be that lucky and the killer was clearly skilled and therefore wouldn't make that kind of mistake.

To walk into a party such as this one and murder a high-profile target without a single person seeing was evidence enough for her.

"Duchess."

Standing, she quickly scanned the floor and found no casing and the bullet was still embedded in his skull. A close-range shot if the powder burns were any indication, which meant he knew his killer.

Slipping out with one last sweep of the room, she closed the door.

"What a shit show."

"Bás says he's handling it and to stay put."

"Then let's go wait with the others."

"You're not gonna mention what you saw earlier?"

Duchess stopped and faced Lotus, regarding her closely. Lotus had a troubled past, a lost mother, lies, murder, coercion, manipulation, and more. Yet Duchess saw the vulnerable woman who lashed out with her tongue because she didn't want to get hurt and it made her want to protect her, but she knew she couldn't always. "Do I need to?"

Lotus tipped her chin mulishly and held her gaze, but Duchess had been doing this job a long time and wouldn't allow her to deflect this with her attitude. "That won't work with me, Lotus. You fucked up and you know it. We both know I don't give a fuck who you sleep with, even if I consider that person a friend. You're both grown-ups but what you don't do is let your guard down on a job. You made yourself vulnerable tonight and that won't be tolerated."

Lotus paled slightly. "What will you do?"

Duchess ground her teeth in an effort not to give in to her instinct to reassure. Lotus needed to learn a hard lesson and perhaps a little fear over her position in Shadow would be enough. She wasn't lying about her and damn, she didn't care and had it been one of the others she'd be reacting the same way. "That's up to Bás but I'll be recommending that you be suspended from active duty until an assessment can be done. You have a death wish, Lotus, and I don't want that on my conscience."

Lotus went to speak but Duchess held up her hand. "This isn't the time or place."

Walking away she hated leaving the woman doubting her place

within Shadow because the truth was, she'd always have one, but whether that was active or not remained to be seen.

In the study she found Damon and Gideon standing near the fireplace, while Marsha sat with a glass of clear liquid in her hand staring into space. Duchess headed towards them quickly.

"How is everyone holding up?"

Gideon reached for her, and she let him take her hand, as Lotus watched on, probably thinking she was a hypocrite, but her head was in the game and that was the difference.

"I can't believe he's dead."

"No, the timing is definitely suspect."

The door opened and four police officers swept into the room. One of them scanned the room, his eyes landing on her and she recognised him instantly. Her lips twitched as Alex Martinez, Eidolon's second in command spoke to Marsha, the police badge he flashed her as fake as the boobs on the woman he spoke to.

"Do you think we'll be held here?"

Duchess shook her head at Gideon's question. "No, Bás has it handled. We'll have to stay a bit but just hang tight."

"Duchess."

She cocked her head to listen to Bás who spoke to her through her earpiece. "Yes?"

"Just play along. Watchdog intercepted the emergency calls, so you have time for Eidolon to clear the scene for us and remove the body and get you out of there."

"I take it the police won't be handling this one?"

"No, they will not."

Duchess moved closer to Gideon, sliding her arm around his waist and nodding for Lotus to resume her role of smitten girlfriend, which she'd been so relishing earlier. Laying her head on Gideon's chest she let him move them away a little so they were standing a few feet away. His arm banded around her waist like an anchor and that's how he made her feel. Stable and secure in a world where everything was on the edge of falling apart.

"You think she did this?"

Duchess followed his line of thought and glanced across the room at Marsha. The woman looked wrecked, her face a mess, her composure torn to shreds. "No, I don't think so. She's competitive and wants to win but I don't think she'd kill her own son over it."

"They were fighting. He told me earlier."

Duchess pursed her lips. "If this was a crime of anger there'd be more destruction, but that scene is clean. This was a professional with a cool head."

"He was scared. When we spoke he was nervous and jumpy. I should have listened and waited with him. Maybe then he'd be alive."

Grief and regret rang out from every pore of the man she knew she was falling in love with. Her heart ached to take this from him but just as he couldn't take her pain she couldn't take his, but she could ease it like he'd done for her. "This isn't your fault, Gideon."

"No, maybe not, but I have to take a share of the blame for who he became."

"No, you don't. You were a child yourself, navigating a complex family life with no instruction manual. Your father is the one to blame."

She looked across at the man who seemed to have aged twenty years since the night began. The look on his face told of regret and the guilt she knew he had the responsibility to bear.

A commotion had Gideon's arms tightening on her, his warmth seeping into her skin as Marsha rose. She stalked toward them and Gideon moved slightly to shield her when she wanted to do the very same to him. Marsha, even if she was the killer and had tried to have Gideon killed, wouldn't be fool enough to do it with witnesses. No, she was savvier than that. Yet as she poked her finger in Gideon's chest, Duchess wondered at the wild look in her eyes.

"You did this." The look she gave him was filled with hate and malice.

Gideon remained calm, holding his hand up to ward off the woman who was attacking. "Calm down, Marsha."

"You killed him, I know you did."

"We both know this wasn't my brother, Marsha, so back off before I explain to the nice police officer watching us who exactly it might be and your involvement in it."

She rounded on Damon, who'd come to his brother's aid so quickly, further cementing his place in Duchess' heart. "You wouldn't dare."

"In a heartbeat."

The fact Damon had no clue who Alex or the others she now recognised as Liam, Blake, and Mitch were, was more evidence of how far he'd go to protect his brother. They were a unit, and they may be different but when the chips turned they were unbreakable.

"I'll kill you for this."

"That's enough, Marsha."

Duchess turned at the harsh sound of Gideon's father who'd joined them.

Marsha turned on him next. "He killed your son. How can you defend him?"

"He did no such thing, and he's my son too. They both are and you'll do well to remember that going forward."

"How could you take his side? Carter is dead. My baby boy is in that room with a bullet in his head."

Her voice cracked and if she'd been an innocent bystander to this Duchess would've felt a smidge of sympathy for her. But she knew how poisonous she was and how she'd been the one to draw her son into her games that, ultimately, ended his life.

"I know he is and my only regret is that I was too weak to stop you from dragging him into this nightmare. If anyone holds responsibility, it's us."

"Get out, get out of my house. I want everyone out of here now." Her high-pitched screech drew the attention of Alex and Mitch. She assumed Liam and Blake were handling the removal of the body and evidence collection.

"Everything alright here, Mrs Cavendish?"

Marsha turned to Alex. "I want these people out of my house."

"We have to clear the scene but as long as they leave their details, we can let these people go home."

Marsha laid her hand on Alex's chest and Duchess could just imagine Evelyn ripping her face off for the violation. Alex removed it smoothly, guiding her to a chair.

"You can leave but give your information to the officer on the door."

"Let's go."

Gideon kept his hand on her back and held her close as they drove back to the safe house in silence. The game had just changed and now they needed to figure out where to go next.

CHAPTER 18

Changed into jeans and a hoodie, Gideon sat opposite his brother and waited for Duchess to come back from where she'd disappeared to with Bás the second she walked back through the door of their warehouse home.

He was still reeling from the conversation with Carter and his murder. His brain went in multiple directions as he tried to figure out how he felt. He kept coming back to the same one though, regret. The things Carter said to him sticking in his gut and twisting.

"This isn't on you, Gideon."

He looked up as Damon pushed a glass of scotch toward him before slugging back his own. "We could have been better brothers to him."

"Yes we could, but she never wanted that. Marsha always wanted that divide and no matter how hard we would have tried, she would've driven the wedge deeper."

"I know." He let the deep flavour of the booze warm his chest as he thought back on his life. "I hated him at first, but when he began to follow us around demanding we play with him or getting in on our games, I grew to love him."

"Same. I was jealous of him, hated that he took dad away from us but then he was a tenacious little fucker, wasn't he?"

"Yeah, he was. Can you remember the time he climbed out the bedroom window after us and was dangling, calling our names?"

Damon chuckled. "Hell yeah. He was only five and we had snuck out to smoke weed behind the greenhouse."

"I thought Dad was going to ground us for the rest of our lives."

"I wish he had. At least then we would've known he gave a shit."

Gideon swirled the liquid in the crystal glass before throwing it back. "She broke him like she broke her son and we let her."

"Is it wrong that I feel so much regret for a man who did so much damage to so many innocents?"

Gideon had been feeling the same way. He shook his head. "I don't know, but I get it. I feel it too."

"I guess it's regret for what could have been."

"Don't live your life thinking like that. It will crush the life out of you, believe me."

Gideon cocked his body toward Hurricane who'd made the statement. "You have regrets?"

The big man laughed without any humour. "More than I can count."

"How do you deal?"

He pulled out a chair and straddled it, his arms laid across the back. "I didn't for a long time but then I realised, with a little help from someone with way more sense than me, that regret does nothing but poison our soul. The only thing we can do is learn and let it shape how we handle our future."

"Wise words, but not simple."

"No, nothing worth doing is ever easy."

He sensed her before he saw her, the air in the room seemed to settle in the same way his heart did. Angling his head back, he saw her walk in beside Bás. Out of the corner of his eye, he saw Damon looking for Lotus, but she was nowhere in sight.

"We have news."

"Should we wait for Lotus, Titan, and Reaper to join us?"

Gideon shook his head. His brother wasn't being as subtle as he thought he was.

"Reaper and Titan will be here shortly, but Lotus won't be joining us for the rest of this mission."

Damon thrust back his chair and glared at Nadia, making Gideon's hackles rise.

"Is this about what you saw?"

Nadia crossed her arms and planted her feet and, despite her being a good eight inches shorter than Damon, she held her own. "No."

"I don't believe you, Duchess."

Gideon rose and stepped toward his brother. "Watch the way you fucking speak to her."

Damon glared between them. "Oh, so it's okay for you two to fuck like rabbits but not anyone else?"

Gideon swung first, his fist hitting his brother in the cheek. Damon dove at him and they crashed to the ground in a tumble of arms and legs, each trying to get a punch in without getting a fist or knee to the face or, worse, the nuts. Gideon rolled and ploughed his fist into his brother's jaw, the next second Damon flipped him and landed a blow to his ribs, knocking the air from him.

"Okay enough, break it up."

Gideon found himself pulled bodily from his brother and watched as Titan held Damon until he settled. Gideon rubbed his bottom lip with his hand smearing blood across his knuckles.

"If you two have finished, I have more serious things to discuss," Bás ground out from between clenched teeth.

"This is bullshit," Damon declared, his heated gaze bouncing off Nadia and him, a look of betrayal on his features he didn't understand.

"What is? What the fuck happened that I don't know about?"

"Lotus and Damon were fucking around in one of the bedrooms when I caught them." Nadia held up a hand to stop Damon and he huffed but remained quiet. "While I don't care who fucks who, I, we, can't have it happen during an operation like the one tonight. Here, where others have our backs, fine but anyone could have walked into that room and shot you both before you had a chance to defend yourselves. Lotus knows that and she knows she fucked up, so she'll be taking a little break to get her shit together."

"So it's okay for you two?"

Damon pointed between them, but Gideon was still reeling that his straight-laced brother had been caught with his pants down. It would have been good to know his brother had found a woman who made him loosen up, even if that woman was scary as fuck, and if the dangers hadn't been shoved down their throats so violently.

"Your brother and I have never put ourselves or any of this team at risk. I get it, Damon, I do but if you care about her at all you'll see this for what it is and not as an attack on you or her."

Damon seemed to lose some of his bluster, and Gideon knew he was smart enough to see the truth. He just wondered if his pride and stubbornness would win out this time.

"Fine. What do we know about Carter?"

Nadia moved to sit beside Bás and he tried not to let that sting. This wasn't about them, it was also her job and she took it seriously. "Well first off, this isn't a police investigation."

Gideon shook his head, his tongue licking out to swipe at the blood where his brother had clocked him. "I don't understand."

"Those men weren't police officers. They're associates of ours. Watchdog intercepted the 999 call. The last thing we need is the authorities involved, especially when we don't know all the players complicit in Project Cradle."

"Makes sense. So what do we know?"

"Hansen killed Carter. What's more, he wanted us to know it. An email came into an unused account of mine about twenty minutes ago. Watchdog is verifying it now but the footage is pretty compelling."

"Why would he do that?"

"It's a warning. He found out Carter was going to flip and killed him for it."

"Why send the video to you?"

"A warning to back off."

"We aren't going to though, are we?"

"No, but I think perhaps I should handle this alone from here on out."

Gideon watched Nadia's jaw tense and knew this wasn't the first time she was hearing this and didn't agree.

"No, we fight as a team. It's where our strength lies."

"I agree," Hurricane nodded.

"You don't understand."

"Because you won't fucking tell us."

"God damn it, Duchess," Bás bellowed, slamming his hand on the desk.

"You know I'm right, Bás."

"He'll come after you all."

"Then we take him down."

"You don't know him like I do."

"Then explain it to me."

For the first time since meeting him, Bás looked rattled. His hand skimmed over his neck in obvious discomfort. Nadia sighed as the silence lengthened.

"Let's get some rest and reconvene in the morning when everyone has a clearer head."

It was almost four am and she was right. Everyone was running on fumes and common sense had taken a hike as evidenced by him and his brother brawling like a couple of five-year-olds in a playground.

He stepped into the room he was sharing with Nadia, any pretence of what they were gone now. Closing the door, she didn't make him wait, just stepped into his arms, her hands rubbing along his back. "Does it hurt?"

He shook his head and gazed down at the woman who'd been his rock when he needed it. She'd taken charge when he was lost, stayed by his side, and knew exactly what he needed. That she wasn't reacting to his fight with Damon spoke volumes. He didn't know many women, if any, that would take a full-blown scrap between brothers in her stride like she had.

"Not really. Nothing we haven't done before. Although not for a while."

"Hot-headed males."

He chuckled. "I guess so."

"Want to talk about it?"

He knew she meant Carter and shook his head.

"Wanna scrub my back in the shower?"

His lips tipped up into a grin and he winced as the cut in his lip split open.

"Ah, poor baby. Come on, let me make you feel better."

Gideon let her lead him into the bathroom and push him so he was leaning against the sink.

"Tell me what you need."

"You." He knew she wanted more but he wasn't lying, he just needed her.

"Be specific."

"Take off your shirt." He watched as she stepped back and pulled her tee over her head, revealing the simple white bra that barely concealed her gorgeous tits.

"Now what?"

Gideon moved from hip to hip as she waited patiently for him to give his next instruction. He knew what this was. She was giving back the control that had been taken so spectacularly tonight. "Now the jeans."

His eyes feasted as she shimmied her jeans down her curvy hips, each movement revealing more to his hungry eyes.

"Now what?"

"Pull your tits out and show me."

His dick was so hard it ached and he palmed it over his jeans as she did what he asked. Her hands cupped the perfect globes in her hands as she tweaked the rosy nipples and offered them up to him.

"Come here."

He reached for her as she stepped closer, his head dipping to capture a perfect peak between his teeth. Her hiss was followed by a moan as he devoured her, sucking and laving until she was squirming in his arms.

His lips skimmed her neck. "On your knees, Nadia."

She sucked in a breath and sank down, her eyes on his cock, hungry as she licked her lips.

"Fuck me, you're perfect."

"Am I?"

"Looking for compliments, Cookie?"

"Maybe."

"Open your mouth, but don't touch me with your hands. I want them behind your back. Can you do that?"

Nadia nodded.

"I need the words, Nadia."

"Yes, sir."

His cock practically wept at the purr in her throat as she called him sir.

Placing her arms behind her back, her tits thrust out rubbing against his thighs and he groaned. Little minx knew exactly what she was doing to him.

He gathered her hair in his hand and gripped it just tight enough to burn and she whimpered.

"You want my cock, baby?"

"God yes."

"Then take it."

Her lips wrapped around his hard length and she sank down until the tip of his crown touched her throat, before hollowing her mouth and sucking. Gideon's eyes rolled back in his head with pleasure.

Her warm, wet mouth was heaven. Her eyes watered as she

worked him, but she never stopped or backed off. His legs felt weak from the sheer fucking pleasure of it all. Her mouth, her submission, the fact she wanted to give him this, cared enough to know what he needed.

His balls drew up and he gave her hair a slight tug to warn her. "I'm going to come, where do you want it?"

Her lips popped free, and she lifted her hand, wrapping it around him and jerking his cock. His vision blacked out for a split second and he thought his knees would buckle if it wasn't for the sink behind him.

"God, I love you, so much."

Her eyes widened and he spilled his seed all over her creamy tits. She let him go as he pulled her and lifted her, before spinning to sit her on the edge of the sink.

"We made a mess."

His finger smoothed his come into her skin, the animal instinct in him wanting to rub his mark into her skin so every fucker knew who she belonged to. "You're a dirty girl."

"I am."

He heard the double entendre and loved this part of her as much as the sweet side he'd seen in Italy. "I meant what I said. I love you, Nadia."

"I love you too."

"If God was making the perfect woman for me, then she is you. You're everything I never knew I wanted"

"Your brother hit you pretty hard, didn't he?"

"Hey, I mean it. Stop ruining my romantic speech."

"I'm not sure it counts as romantic if your come is drying on my tits, Gideon."

"It is if it's us."

"I guess it is."

"Now, it's time for me to repay the favour and as much as I love the idea of you walking around with my brand on your skin, I have a feeling it might not feel so fun for you. So, let's get in the shower and I can scrub your back and clean you before I dirty you up again."

"Sounds like a great idea."

He stripped bare before stepping into the shower and, shielding her from the cold water until it warmed up, he took the time to wash her hair and clean her body, paying extra special attention to all his favourite parts.

When they were both spent, he carried her to bed, where he made love to her again before falling asleep with her body spread over him like a blanket. Today had been rough but with her beside him, he could cope with anything.

CHAPTER 19

"I thought I might find you here."

Bás' spine stiffened as she walked into the weapons room of the safe house. If it could even be called that. "What do you need?"

Her best skill was reading people, of knowing what they needed. In the beginning with Gideon, it had been tricky. She couldn't read him because she was too caught up in fighting her attraction to him. Now though, it was as if she could anticipate what he wanted. But unlike with most people, it went both ways between them. He did the same, not giving her what she thought she needed but what she actually needed before she even knew it.

She'd left him in bed this morning, wiped out from the hell of the evening before but she hoped she'd given him back a small measure of the control he needed to thrive. Now she needed to do the same for her boss but without sharing her heart, which she knew belonged to Gideon and always would.

"Can we sit?"

He sighed and laid down the gun he'd been cleaning. Taking a seat, he faced her as she placed her clasped hands on the table.

"Talk to me, Bás."

He looked at his hands not facing her. "About what?"

Duchess was stubborn too, so she waited for him to look at her and when he did, she saw the anguish in his eyes. "Tell me about Hansen. How did you two meet?"

A sigh that seemed to be dragged from the very depths of hell swept from his chest. "What does it matter, it's ancient history."

"Come on, Bás, you don't believe that any more than I do. This is personal for you and for him too, and we need to know why if we're going to fight him. We could have lost Lotus tonight and now he's toying with us."

The video Hansen had sent of him killing Carter hadn't been the only thing. He'd also sent a video of Lotus and Damon, and he was close enough that he could have killed them both before they'd had a chance to react. His threat had been clear. He could have killed her and hadn't, but only Bás knew why this game was afoot.

"She was stupid to let her guard down. We've taught her better than that."

"She was and we have, but we both know that human beings aren't that simple. She made a mistake, a bad one, yes but she's human like we all are."

"She's reckless."

"And so is what you're proposing by going after Hansen alone."

"It's different."

"Then tell me why."

His hands clenched and unclenched the knuckles almost white, and she knew how hard this was for him.

"If I tell you it stays between us, but you won't change my mind."

Nadia nodded and sat silent while he explained his background with Hansen. How they'd met, their relationship, everything all the way back to his childhood. When he was done, Nadia felt shell-shocked by what she now knew.

He was right, when that particular cat was out of the bag there was no putting it back inside, no matter how much they'd want too.

"Now do you get why I didn't want to say anything to anyone?"

"I do, but I'm not anyone, Bás. I'm here to have your back and I can do that better now I know what's at stake and what he knows."

"Maybe, but nobody else."

"Listen, they'll understand it won't change the way they see you."

His features hardened and she could see why he had the feared reputation he did. She and the team sometimes forgot that Bás was Gaelic for death. He'd earned his nickname the hard way and now she understood him just a little more. She just wished he'd give that insight to the others.

"I mean it, Duchess, don't make me regret telling you."

"I would never break your confidence, Bás, but I won't let you do this alone either. We're a team, and our biggest strength is each other. You preach it so you better believe it."

"I do that's why I can't let him break us. If I go after him alone, the team stays safe."

Duchess laughed and threw up her hands. "Don't be so naïve. The team is at risk already."

"Maybe you're right."

"You know I am."

"Whose idea was it to employ you?"

Duchess laughed. "If I remember rightly, you said you wouldn't do this without me."

"I must have had one too many concussions."

"Well, that's definitely true, but seriously, you employed me because you knew I wouldn't be afraid to call you out on your bullshit and that's what this is now, utter bull crap."

"Haven't you got a boyfriend to go bother?"

"I'm not sure that's what he is."

"You fucking?"

"Yes, not that it's any of your business."

"He go with you when your ma died?"

"Yes?"

"You say the L word yet?"

"Maybe."

"You see where I'm going with this?"

"Fine, we're together but I'm not sure it has a future despite all that. His family is still a hot mess and trying to bury him and his company. We still have Project Cradle to deal with and he's a businessman and I'm, well, not that."

"If you want it enough you can make it work. Look at Reaper and Lucía. Hell, if that can work so can you and the suit."

"Let's take it a day at a time. First things first, we need to touch base with Jack and find out what he knows from the scene."

He pointed a finger at her. "Good plan. Why didn't I think of that?"

"Jerk."

"You know I've killed people for less than name-calling."

"You can't kill me. You need me to be the buffer between you and the team."

"True."

"Now, let's go rattle some cages and see what today brings us."

"More carnage no doubt."

"You love the carnage."

"I did, but I'm growing tired of it all. Don't you ever want a quieter life?"

"Every damn day."

"Then why do we do it, Duchess?"

"The world needs us. They just don't know it and if not us, then who? Plus, we'd get bored within ten minutes if we retired."

"You might be right, but maybe we should look at recruiting some more members. I'm getting too old for this shit."

"You're not even forty yet."

"Close enough and my body feels one hundred and fifty."

She slapped him in the gut. "Time to get in the gym, old man."

"Fuck you. I could still whoop anyone of you."

"Who wants a whooping?" Hurricane asked from where he was leaning on the door.

"Yeah, not you. Even I know my limits."

Duchess left Bás talking with Hurricane, satisfied that she knew enough to keep her team safe—for now.

CHAPTER 20

His eyes tracked her as Nadia paced around the room. The morning had seen much less action than he'd expected after last night. The team, minus Lotus, were waiting around as information began to trickle into them. He hated to admit it but the atmosphere lacked a certain something without the snippy Lotus to give them all shit.

Damon sat beside him and Gideon smirked, seeing the black eye.

"Dick."

"Jerk-off."

"Oh, go boil your head."

Gideon laughed and then hissed as his lips split again.

"Serves you right."

"Maybe it does but I won't stand for anyone speaking to her like that, not even you, brother."

Gideon followed Nadia's movements as she spoke with Titan, her hands moving animatedly.

"So it's the real deal? She isn't just one of your playthings?"

Gideon huffed out a laugh. "Nope, she's the one."

"Wow, I never thought I'd see the day my big brother, the playboy, got taken off the market in such dramatic fashion."

"Me either, but I love her."

Damon slugged him in the shoulder, but his eyes were on the woman who commandeered his every thought. "I'm happy for you."

"Yeah, well, hold that thought. It's not like we've discussed our future."

"You will. Duchess is a great woman."

A flare of jealousy toward his brother made his gut tighten but he pushed it away. Damon and Nadia were friends, nothing more.

"She is, but she's also fucking amazing at this job. Is it fair to ask her to give this up and be with me?"

"Or now, hear me out, you could walk away from Cavendish for her."

Gideon gave his brother his full attention, the idea never having crossed his mind. "And do what?"

"I don't know, grow tomatoes? Write a book, knit, windsurf, how the fuck should I know? My point is you can do whatever you want."

All his life he'd been groomed for this role, he enjoyed it but did he love it? "Well, it's moot until we fix this mess."

Bás strode into the middle of the room and Nadia came to his side, planting herself behind him, but he needed her closer and hooked her around the waist and pulled her onto his lap. It was a risk, she might just castrate him for being so forward in front of her friends, but she didn't. She smiled and kissed his cheek. Hurricane and Reaper bumped fists with a grin, but nobody said a word.

"Listen up."

The room went silent, the air stilling, almost like the sky before a tornado blew through.

"I have a few pieces of information to share with the team."

Each of them looked calm, not bored exactly but not like Bás was imparting news and he suspected they already knew and this was for him and Damon.

"We have confirmed that Melissa Green is in fact Marsha's daughter."

"How?"

Bás canted his head. "DNA doesn't lie, my friend."

"We also have evidence that Carter was blackmailing Tarquin with telling Melissa, who we believe is just a normal woman who thinks her life is all sunshine and rainbows."

"Does that put her in danger?"

"Yes, which is why Titan is heading to the US to offer security. He'll meet with Tarquin, and we hope to gain his support and allow us to gather as much intel as we can from him about Marsha."

"Can't we just arrest her now?"

"No." Bás shook his head but Gideon was distracted by the woman playing with the back of his neck where his hair met his collar. She shifted and it made things worse, his dick hardening beneath her thighs.

Bending his head, he spoke into her neck. "Stop teasing or I'm going to bend you over this table and fuck the sexy ass that's torturing me." A hitch met his ears and he almost groaned, she was fucking turned on by the thought. "Fuck me, you want that."

"So, as I was saying, we'll visit Marsha and speak with her, but I want everyone on alert. As far as we know Hansen is still in London and he won't hesitate to come after any one of us."

Duchess moved to stand, and he held her hips tight keeping her in place. "If you move, the whole room is going to get a show of exactly what you do to me."

The others dispersed, leaving them alone, and he wished he had more time, just the two of them to explore everything between them. He couldn't get enough of her and doubted he ever would.

"Is that a fact?"

He pinched her ass and she yelped.

"Ow."

"That's for teasing me."

"Me teasing you? You were the one whispering dirty thoughts in my ear."

"Because you kept wriggling that sweet ass on my dick."

"It is a sweet ass, isn't it?"

Gideon palmed the sexy curve as she looped her arms over his shoulders.

"It sure is and when I get you alone, I'm going to fuck it while you play with those gorgeous tits."

"Jesus, Gideon. Warn a girl before you go all alpha porn star on her."

Gideon laughed and kissed her, not with the heady passion he was feeling but with a playfulness he'd never experienced with another woman. He slapped her ass. "Get up, this isn't working to tame my dick."

She smoothed her hair and laughed. "Well, hurry up because we're paying a visit to stepmother dearest."

Gideon sobered and his hard-on deflated like a popped balloon. "We are?"

"Yes. Pay attention in class, Gideon."

He followed her toward the garages like a puppy on a leash and didn't even care how pussy whipped he was. "I would if you wouldn't distract me."

She took his chin in her hands and kissed him before tugging on his bottom lip. "Sorry, I'll make it up to you later."

"Not helping, Cookie."

Nadia laughed as she climbed in the back seat, with Hurricane and Bás in the front.

The drive to his childhood home was uneventful, the mood shifting the closer they got. He'd learned Damon was heading to the US with Titan to help pave the way with Tarquin and Melissa but not until they had more intel. He had no idea who was running his company right now. He hadn't opened his laptop in days or replied to any of the hundreds of messages from his directors, except to say he had a family issue and they had to handle things for a few days.

Lucky for him, he'd picked a great team, except for one or two who were lower level and didn't have access to anything of importance. Watchdog had cleared them too, which added weight to his decision to let them be until this was less of a precarious position.

The grounds were quiet in the harsh light of day, everything looked the same and yet a big piece of his life was gone. He'd hated Carter at the end, despised the way he'd tried to ruin them all and him especially, but he'd always live with his brother's last words in his head. Had he been trying to change or was it all a ruse to trick him into exposing himself? He'd never know now.

His father met them at the door, and he looked to have aged twenty years overnight. His face was sallow, his eyes sunken, thick black circles beneath. He looked broken and no matter what had gone on, he'd lost a son last night and the child in him hated to see him that way.

"Thanks for coming, Gideon."

Gideon clasped his father's shoulder and squeezed gently. "How you holding up?"

"Standing just about. I know he had his faults, but he was my son and I loved him, just as I do you and Damon."

Gideon pursed his lips, remaining silent as his father lead them into the study.

"Marsha will be down shortly. I'm going to take a walk in the garden if you don't need me."

"I'll come and find you before we leave."

His dad nodded, his whole body seeming to sag under the weight he was carrying. "I'd like that."

He nodded his head at Nadia. "Look after him."

"I will." She slipped her hand through his and he stepped closer to her. His father hadn't meant it in a physical way, he'd meant emotionally. Little did he know this woman was proficient at both.

"He needs you."

Gideon glanced down at Nadia as she spoke and knew she was thinking of her own mother. "I know, I'm just not sure if I can get past everything that's happened and go back to what we were."

"Then don't. Move forward and find a new normal for you to build on."

"How did I get so lucky to find you?"

Her lips quirked up. "I honestly don't know. You must have done something good in a former life."

Her sass and confidence, coupled with the vulnerable side she only showed a very few, drew him in with every breath he took until he found himself so gone for her, that if she said she wanted the moon on a stick he'd find a way to give it to her.

He stopped himself from saying it as Marsha walked into the room. A cream velvet lounge suit and her hair in a sleek bun on her head her only nod to her usual put-together appearance.

"What do you want?" Her scathing look travelled over him and until his dying day he'd never understand what his father saw in her.

"We want to talk to you about Tarquin Green."

Marsha went as white as a ghost at Bás' demand. Her legs seemed to give way and she sat heavily in the wingback chair she'd occupied the previous night. Hurricane wandered off with a nod to Nadia and he moved toward the fireplace, drawn by the pictures. Nadia sat opposite Marsha and Bás was off to one side.

"I haven't heard that name in years."

"We understand you were friends."

Marsha smiled and it reminded him of his brother's sixth birthday when she'd made them all dress up as pirates for his party and she'd taken a picture, her smile sad even then.

"We were. He was my best friend and my first love."

"You had his child."

Marsha's eyes flashed up in shock and fear showed on her face. "I…"

"We know about Melissa."

Marsha sagged as if life had truly been sucked from her. "Is she safe?"

Bás chose not to answer that but mined for more information. "Did you know Carter was blackmailing Tarquin?"

Her head shot up and he wasn't sure he believed the lie that fell from her lips. "Of course not. Carter didn't know about Melissa." The woman looked terrified, her hand shaking as she ripped a tissue in her hands to shreds.

"Does Melissa know about you?"

Gideon frowned, Bás knew she didn't.

"No, she has no idea and it needs to stay that way."

"Why?"

Her eyes glittered with tears. "Because I don't trust them and it's the only way she stays safe."

"Who don't you trust?"

She threw up her hands. "The people in charge of Project Cradle. I assume that's why you're really here."

"Let's talk about that. Who's in charge of the organisation? Is it Hansen?"

"He is the fixer. He keeps everything running smoothly. He's the top man's pet."

"Does this person have a name?"

Marsha huffed out a laugh with no mirth in it at all, her head shaking.

"Marsha, this person likely killed your son and if he finds out about Melissa, she could be next."

She cocked her head towards Nadia and his instinct to move closer and draw her attention away was strong.

"Do you have any idea why I got involved with the project?"

"Greed?"

Marsha smirked. "I wish it had been but it was ambition. I wanted to prove to my father I was worthy of him. That I wasn't the screw-up he thought I was. The project had been his but the government shut it down when they found out he was forcing women to enter it."

"Did he force you?"

Tears glinted in her eyes but she blinked them away. "Yes. I wanted to marry Tarquin and keep my child but he dumped me. Said he wanted nothing to do with me. I found out later my father had paid him off with the promise of custody of my daughter."

"You wanted to keep her?"

"Of course I wanted to keep her."

"Why didn't you fight for her?"

"Don't be naive. You don't fight men like my father, especially when they have men like Hansen to keep you in line. So I turned it to my advantage. I said I'd work with them, help them build something better. The clinics were my idea and they worked perfectly until Carter got cold feet."

"So your father is in charge."

She shook her head.

Gideon saw her open her mouth but before she could voice the name, blood exploded from the side of Marsha's head, covering Nadia in a crimson river of death.

CHAPTER 21

"So that's it?"

Duchess waited for Bás to look at her and accepted the nod when he did.

"We've cleared Winston Cavendish of any involvement in Project Cradle and that's all we're here for."

"What about Elysian?"

"The Casinos are legitimate."

Duchess paced the length of the warehouse. It had been two days since Marsha had been shot dead just seconds before revealing who the top man at Project Cradle was. The team had found bugs and cameras all over the house and Watchdog was still trying to trace where the footage was sent with no luck so far.

"We both know that's not entirely true, they're up to their necks in illegal activity."

"Yes, but the man behind that enterprise is dead and so is his mother. Damon and Gideon can't go undercover and take it up because we know Hansen is onto them working with us."

She didn't say it but she had absolutely no intention of letting them either. "So, what? We head back to Hereford and keep digging?"

"Yes. We do our jobs and this portion of it is over."

Duchess chewed the cuticle on her pinkie until it bled and then stilled, realising Bás had stopped what he was doing and was watching her, his arms folded over his chest as he waited.

"What?"

"What's this really about?"

"Nothing. I'm just not sure we're done here."

"The team or you?"

He was calling her out and she hated that she was so easy to read. "Both."

"Hansen has left the country, Marsha is dead, Carter is dead. We have a wealth of new information to go through now we've seized everything from both mother and son and Winston is in protective custody."

"I still think Gideon and Damon should be too."

"We offered, but they both refused. Honestly, I don't think they're in any danger now."

She didn't necessarily agree with that. "Disagree."

"Why?"

"Damon has flown halfway around the world to smooth the way with Melissa for Titan."

"True. Do you think Tarquin is the top man Marsha talked about?"

"I don't know. Marsha seemed frightened of that person, but she called Tarquin her first love and seemed to get a faraway look when he was mentioned, so that doesn't track." She crossed her arms and sighed. "You know we could send Lotus to have his back."

Bás jaw flexed as his brows drew low. "He has Titan."

"Titan is there for Melissa's safety, not Damon's."

"I don't know. She was taken off this case because she and Damon were thinking with their genitals, not their heads."

Duchess gave a mock shiver. "Please don't say genitals again, it creeps me out."

"Whatever."

"So can I send her?"

"Has she completed the mandated sessions we required?"

"I spoke to Peyton and she's happy it was just a slip because of the anniversary of her mother's death."

"Poor kid. She's had a shit time."

Duchess thought back to their conversation and it shed a little more light on why Bás allowed Lotus to get away with so much. "She has but so have a lot of people."

"Fine, send her but this is on you. If she fucks up this time you can clean up the mess."

"You know who can keep her in line?"

"Rykov."

"Rykov." They both said together.

"Yes, and he's finished with his situation in Russia. Perhaps we can bring him on full-time now."

"You think him and Damon with Lotus is a good idea?"

"I do. Rykov can handle her."

"But can he handle seeing her with Damon?"

"It doesn't matter, does it? They can't be together."

Duchess cocked her head. "You know that's more of a suggestion than a rule, Bás."

He pointed a finger at her face. "Don't."

"What? I was just going to ask where Val was?"

"She's in Germany checking out a breeding program for the dogs."

"Uh-huh."

"Get out of here and figure out if you're coming back to Hereford or not."

Duchess felt like she'd been slapped. "Why would I not?"

"Because lover boy lives here and you two can't stay away from each other."

"I'd never leave the team, Bás, not when they need me."

"We do need you, but it's time to put yourself first for a change."

Duchess shook her head. "That's not how I work and you know it."

He stepped close and tipped her chin up, so she was looking him in the eyes. He was like the brother she didn't have. Family had always been a strange construct to her, never having that closeness but here within Shadow she'd found it. Losing her mother made her treasure it more.

"Duchess, you don't need to make yourself indispensable to part of this team. You'll always, no matter what, have a place with us. We're not going anywhere."

Tears clogged her throat and she nodded. "I know." And she did. They had never needed her, they wanted her and while she was excellent at her job, they would cope without her. What she couldn't discern was if she could cope with not being needed.

"Go talk to Gideon."

He'd been in back-to-back meetings since Marsha's death. His father had up and signed over the company to him and Damon, walking away without a backward glance. "He's probably fired his new PA."

"Most likely."

Duchess decided to head to Cavendish Enterprises but wanted to stop by and clear her apartment first. She'd decided to sell it. She owned the place in Italy since her mother's death and the restaurant there too. She knew Naples wasn't her home, but it was a place she loved to visit. One that brought back echoes of happy memory but also held a resentment she'd never shake. In her head, her mother had chosen it over her. And while the link to her mum was nice to have, she knew she'd never live there.

She'd get a manager in to run it and lease the apartment above it. That and selling this place would give her a cushion in the future. God knew she couldn't do this forever and she wanted a family of her own one day.

Packing her clothes and a few personal items, she labelled the boxes in a thick black marker, which she'd have delivered to the pub. Hereford was her home now but when she thought of home she couldn't separate it from Gideon. In a short time, he'd become her safe place, but was he her future?

He had everything in London. His home, his company, which he'd worked so tirelessly for, and his brother. She could move here if he wanted but for just once in her life, she wanted someone to choose her. To put her front and centre like she did others.

Having procrastinated enough, she called a cab and made her way to the office she'd called home on and off for the past year. Tipping her head back, she looked up at the magnificent building with the Cavendish name and logo on it. She'd stopped seeing Gideon as the master of a billion-pound enterprise and begun to see him as a man she loved. Who made her feel like the centre of his world without asking her to dim her own light. Duchess had always been confident and outgoing but she was self-aware enough to know that it hid some serious insecurities about people.

Shaking off the melancholy, she headed inside, waving to Jimmy, the security guard. The ride up was long and her nerves began to jangle as if she was going to jump off the building, not go and speak to the man she loved and who said he loved her.

When the doors opened, she saw the new PA crying outside the door to Gideon's office as she cleared her desk. She could hear him inside yelling at someone and it almost brought a smile to her face. It was so reminiscent of the scene that had met her the day she'd started there under Damon's employ.

Stopping, she shoved one hand into the pocket of her jeans and tapped her knuckle on the woman's desk. Big blue eyes looked at her mascara leaking down her face.

"Who's he in with?"

"Tom Lockett, although not for long."

"Can I go in?"

"You can swing from the lighting for all I care. That man is a pig and he can stick his job up his ass. Nothing is worth this shit."

With that, the woman grabbed her bag and walked away with as much dignity as she could muster. Pushing open the door, she poked her head in and saw Gideon with his jacket off, shirt sleeves rolled up his forearms, and his tie undone, glaring at Tom with his hands on his hips. He looked magnificent, like a King or a warrior about to head into battle. His features swathed with determination, he looked so handsome her heart clenched.

"Get out of my office, Tom. You're fired."

"This isn't the end of this, Gideon."

"Yes, it is. You were passing on confidential information to my brother about things I specifically told you not to. That's corporate espionage and holds a jail sentence. So go ahead and test me."

"Fucking prick."

Gideon spied her and gestured to her to come inside.

"Not the first time I've heard that and you're definitely not the most attractive. Now get out."

Tom glared at her as he slammed past her, yanking the door closed so hard it shook the hinges. He opened his arms and she walked right into them, tipping her head up for his kiss. He obliged, a growl moving up his throat when she wound her fingers into his hair, her nails scoring his scalp.

"I missed you."

She patted his chest. "You saw me this morning."

"See, too long ago, that's almost eight hours."

"I see your PA walked out."

"She did?" He gave her an adorable look of confusion before shrugging.

"She did."

"Oh. You want to come back and help me wrangle this lot into place?"

She sat down in the chair facing his desk and he leaned his ass against the desk beside her. "That's why I'm here."

"Oh?"

"It's time for me to go home."

"To your place in London?"

Duchess rolled her lips between her teeth. "No, back to Hereford."

Gideon folded his arms across his chest, and it took everything in her not to drool. The man was stacked and beautiful and she loved him, but she couldn't stay.

"What about us?"

She lifted a shoulder. "I don't know."

"Don't you love me?"

"Gideon, come on. You know I do, but my job is there and they need me."

"I see. So, you won't stay if I ask?"

"You could move to Hereford? You've always said this wasn't your dream."

"I can't just walk away, Nadia. I have thousands of people who rely on me."

"So do I."

"Then I guess we're at a stalemate."

She stood and her heart felt like it was cracking and bleeding all over his floor. "I guess so."

"You can't ask me to give this up, Nadia."

It was on the tip of her tongue to tell him that she shouldn't have to. If he really loved her, he'd walk away without a backward glance. She knew she was being a hypocrite but for once she wanted to come first. "I would *never* ask that." Raising on her tiptoes, she kissed his cheek, closing her eyes as his scent bled into her psyche and the feel of him against her lips marked her soul for all eternity. "Goodbye, Gideon."

She battled the tears as she walked to the door, silently begging him to stop her. Yet the silence continued, and no hand reached for her, no sound of her name being called filled her ears. Her last sight as the lift doors closed was of Gideon closing his office door on her.

CHAPTER 22

He'd thought he'd experienced every pain known to man in the last few weeks but having the woman he loved walk away from him was like nothing he could imagine. His pride had kept him from begging, but he knew deep down it never would have worked anyway.

If there was one thing he knew about Nadia, it was that once her mind was made up she saw it through. His office door opened on the third day since the light had left his world and two women he didn't know walked into the room.

"Excuse me, do I know you?"

He could see now that both were pregnant, the shorter blonde one not too far along but the taller of the two with short brown hair was, he guessed, close to popping.

"Nope, not exactly, but we know you. You heart-breaking, spirit-killing demon."

Gideon sat back not entirely sure what to say or do. "Sorry?"

The blonde, who was five foot three if she was lucky, leaned over his desk and he found himself leaning back at the fire in her eyes.

"You should be, scuz bucket. If I had my way, I'd string you up by your balls and when those fuckers fell off I'd put them into a casserole for Monty and Scout."

"Who in God's name are you?"

The taller one leaned in then. "Your worst nightmare, asshole."

"That's it, I'm calling security."

Gideon picked up the phone to call his security team and fire them all for letting these two maniacs into his office when the door burst open. Two men stalked in with deadly, furious looks aimed at the two women.

"You call this baby shopping, Charlie?"

"Busted."

"Snow, what the hell? You said you were meeting Charlie for coffee."

"We had coffee first."

The man, who wore a three-piece suit and looked very familiar, growled. "Don't split hairs with me, Snow."

"He needed telling."

"You need to mind your own business, Charlie, and you too, Snow."

The blonde they were calling Snow glared at him. "See what you did?"

"Me?" Gideon pointed to his chest. "You barged into my office like a pair of deranged mental patients issuing threats."

The suit pointed a warning finger at him. "Watch how you speak to my wife."

"Then get your wife out of my office."

Charlie shook her head. "What the hell did Duchess see in you?"

"You know Nadia?" His heart beat ten to the dozen and snippets of conversation began to filter through. Nadia had mentioned two of her colleagues and friends were expecting.

"Yeah, we're her family."

"How is she?"

Snow sniffed, throwing her hair over her shoulder in disdain. "Like you care."

"I care. I love her."

"If you love her, genius, why the fuck are you here in this boring ivory tower while she breaks her heart over you in Hereford?"

"I asked her to stay."

The man placed his arm around her, a tender look on his face. "Snow, watch your blood pressure."

Gideon swept both his hands through his hair and began to pace along the window. The sight of London below, once something he loved, was now just a dull reminder of what he'd lost. Everywhere he looked was a reminder of her and what he'd lost.

"He's too stupid to live." Charlie let the man he guessed was her husband lead her to a chair before he took up a position at her back.

"What the hell was I supposed to do?"

The two men looked at each other and he thought he saw an inkling of sympathy but also a hefty dose of derision.

"Fight for her, douche dick."

"How?"

"Sit down, your pacing is making me sick, and I don't want to puke on your pristine carpet."

Gideon sat on the chair closest to Snow, giving her his full attention as he waited for her to impart life-changing knowledge to him.

"Do you really love her? Like, lie down in front of a stampeding herd of elephants for her love?"

"Yes."

"Would you do that for anyone else, or anything else?"

"No." He mentally apologised to Damon, but it was the truth.

"Now do you get it?"

Gideon frowned. "No."

"Jesus Christ, man. Don't be so dumb. Sell this place or get a manager in and get your ass to Hereford. She needs you to choose her, over everything." The man behind Charlie threw up his hands as if he was talking to someone dumber than shit.

"Because nobody else ever has."

"Oh, maybe we spoke too soon, I think he's finally getting it."

Charlie patted her husband's arm in excitement and he ignored her, the root of an idea forming.

As epiphanies went it was a long time coming. He should have seen this the day she'd walked in and asked him about their future. It was never a contest. He'd just been blinded by responsibility and the misconception that this was what he'd always wanted when it wasn't.

"I need to make a call."

He ignored the group who were now bickering amongst themselves about trackers and trust and picked up his phone. He had plans to make and the love of his life to win back.

Two long days later, he was stepping into a pub called The Crown, the low ceiling, wood and brass bar, and rich reds of the décor gave it a quintessential English feel. Every head in the packed bar turned to look at him, but he only had eyes for one person.

"Gideon?"

He drank in the sight of her like a man who'd been stranded in the desert for months. God, she was beautiful. Even with shadows under her eyes, she was the most stunning creature he'd ever laid eyes on.

"Hey." He kept his hands in his pockets knowing he wouldn't be able to resist the urge to reach for her if they weren't.

"What are you doing here? Is Damon okay?"

That was so typical of the woman he loved to think of others before ever factoring in that someone would come for her and he, like the asshole he was, had strengthened her belief that she wasn't enough. "Everyone is fine."

Her nose wrinkled and she frowned, her head shaking slightly as if she was trying to clear her confusion. "Is something wrong?"

"Yes."

The bar was silent as each person listened into the conversation and he didn't care, he'd shout what he had to say from the rooftops.

She grasped his biceps and even that little touch sent his heart into his throat.

"What? Tell me?"

"I can't sleep, I can't eat. I've taken to wearing grey joggers all day every day just because it makes me think of you. You're not with me and it's wrong. This isn't how it should be."

Her lips wobbled and she blinked hard, and he was done keeping his hands off her. He stepped into her space and looped his arms around her hips, drawing her close so not even a gnat could get between them. "I've missed you so damn much."

A tear broke free and rolled down her cheek and he knew he'd chop his own balls off before he caused her another.

He thumbed it away and took her lips gently. "Don't cry, Cookie. Don't ever cry over me."

"I miss you too."

"Well, that stops now."

"How so?"

"I sold Cavendish Enterprises. I'm now officially jobless and in ten days' time I'll be homeless."

"You what?"

Her screech was louder than he expected, and he chuckled as he lifted her off her feet and slowly swung her around. "I realised, with the help of some people who love you almost as much as I do, that you're my home. I belong wherever you are."

"We love her more, bozo."

He chuckled as Duchess looked over his shoulder toward Snow before raising her eyebrows. "Is this real?"

"As real as it gets. I can't live without you, Nadia. Please don't make me."

"I can't believe you sold the company that you worked so hard for, just for me."

He rubbed his nose against her cheek. "I'd do anything for you. Even lie in front of a herd of stampeding elephants."

"Random."

He chuckled. "I'll explain later."

He dipped his head and took her lips in a kiss where he let every ounce of emotion for her free. He made a promise to her and himself in that kiss that he'd never leave her or make her feel less again.

"I love you, Nadia."

"I love you too, you big oaf."

"Wow, now the insults start? Okay, I can take it."

"Come meet my friends."

He let her lead him toward the throng of people, some he knew and others only by sight. But all of them loved her, just none as much as he did. As soon as he could plan it, he was going to pop the question and nail this down because he was never going to risk losing her again.

∽

"Miss Rose, are you sure it says to put this much sugar in the recipe?"

He didn't know what he'd been thinking but since the night three months ago when he'd arrived here in Longtown to throw himself on the mercy of the woman who completed him, he'd been accepted in a way he hadn't seen coming.

Bás had offered to introduce him to a friend called Zack Cunningham, who was looking for someone to help him diversify his portfolio. Gideon loved the idea of being a consultant and going where he was needed but having the freedom to move on or walk away when it didn't suit him any longer.

"Yes, yes. Now, add the brown sugar too."

Miss Rose was ninety if she was a day and held court in the pub most nights. Some said she had a gift for predicting things and Bishop, the husband of the now very pregnant Charlie, said she'd seen him and Charlie getting back together before he had. He knew each of these couples' stories and the fight they'd had to get where they were and, while his and Nadia's was far from the most violent, it was his favourite.

"Good. Now mix it but don't over-mix it."

Twenty minutes later, the kitchen of the home he and Duchess had purchased on the outskirts of the village smelled divine.

"Now, you can't ice it until it's cooled."

"Thank you for helping me." He'd been determined to do this himself until he realised he couldn't bake for shit and hadn't wanted to ask Nadia's friends for help. He loved them mostly, even Lotus, but they couldn't keep secrets like these for shit. Tell them a top-secret nuclear launch code and they'd take it to the grave under torture. Give them gossip and their lips flapped like a clean load of washing in spring.

"It's my pleasure and I'm just gonna put this out there now. When those twins come along, Rose is a nice name."

"Twins?" He could feel the blood draining from his face.

Her cackle and the smooth skin of her gnarled hand eaten up with arthritis patted his face. "Don't worry, Giddy up, it won't be this year but soon. You mark my words."

Hours later, the idea of twins with Nadia's face and his eyes running around their home was still on his mind as he waited for her to come home. Looking out of the window, he saw her car draw up and pull into the drive. Taking a deep breath, he walked to the kitchen to check on dinner. The lasagne he'd made was his one signature dish and thankfully Nadia loved it. Her father had taught him to cook it when he'd visited a few months ago.

Seeing them speak over each other in multiple different languages drove home just how damn smart this woman was and how lucky he was to have her in his life.

"Honey, I'm home."

Gideon rushed to the door and saw the grin on her face as she shucked off her jacket.

"That never gets old, baby."

He handed her a glass of red wine and ushered her into the open-plan living area where he'd set up the table with candles and flowers.

"What's all this?"

"Can't a man spoil the woman he loves without the third degree?"

Her lips tipped up and she rose on her toes to kiss him, the flavour of the wine sweet on her lips. "He can."

She sat at the table, and he rushed back to pull the lasagne out of the oven, almost burning himself as he juggled the pan.

"Need some help?"

He could hear the smile in her voice and shot her a look that promised retribution.

Her giggle only made him smile. "What am I going to do with you?"

Placing the pan on the potholder in the centre of the table, he replied. "I could think of one or two things."

Gideon dished out two servings of the dinner, regretting the decision to eat before going through with this. He'd faced corporate raiders, gunmen, his evil stepmother, and Lotus with a hangover, and he'd never been this nervous.

"So tell me about your day?"

He listened as she told him about her day spent with Bás going through potential new recruits for Shadow. Since becoming a permanent part of Nadia's life, he'd signed an NDA which meant nothing since the organisation didn't exist but the threat Jack, the man behind it all, had issued had been real enough.

Gideon could respect that and understood the need for such secrecy. He didn't mind, he had no intention of going anywhere ever.

"You not hungry?"

Gideon looked down at his half-eaten plate and the mangled mess where he'd just moved the food around the plate. "I made dessert."

"You did?"

He got up to go grab the box with the giant cookie he'd made, tapping his pocket to reassure himself the ring was still there.

Instead of taking his seat, he stopped beside Nadia's chair, and she turned her body toward him. The skin of her thigh brushed his knuckles. She had the softest skin imaginable, and he never failed to be awed by her beauty.

Angling the box towards her, he saw the question in her eyes but as always, she waited for him to speak, patient from the first to the last.

"Nadia, the first time I met you, I felt something that shocked me. I pushed it away because it terrified me. You're clever, kind, and breathtakingly beautiful. You challenge me in ways I never could have expected and make each day an adventure. I thought that falling in love with you was the scariest thing I'd ever done, but it's not. The most frightening, heart-stopping thought is not spending every day for the rest of my life waking up beside you. Of loving you and having you love me back." He took a breath and opened the box. "I love you, Nadia. Will you marry me?"

Her eyes watered and her hands covered her mouth but they dropped to the box where a giant cookie had the words 'will you marry me' piped in icing.

"Did you make this?"

"I did. Miss Rose helped me."

"Oh, Gideon." She took the box and placed it on the table and then threw her body over him, tumbling them to the floor, where he held her.

"Is that a yes or a hell no?"

"Of course I'll marry you."

His lips found hers and he kissed her there on the floor and only hours later, after he'd made love to her, did he remember the ring.

"Shit." He hopped out of bed and ran down the stairs naked to grab his discarded trousers.

"How did it go, lover boy?"

The sound that came out of his mouth was the unmanliest sound he'd ever made.

"Lotus, what the fuck?" His hands came to cover his cock and he backed up toward the door.

She was sitting at his kitchen table eating the leftover lasagne. "Did she say yes?"

"Yes. Jesus, get out of my house."

Lotus nodded. "Good, good. Now, you treat her right or next time you'll only need one hand to cover that package."

He watched her pick up the pan and disappear through his back patio door with a wave. That woman had serious boundary issues and the man who won her heart would need to have balls of steel.

"Is everything all right?"

He turned to see Nadia wearing one of his shirts. It fell to her thighs, open from neck to tail and he thought she'd never looked sexier. Grabbing his trousers, he dug the ring from the pocket and sank to one knee. "I forgot the ring. So for the second time, will you marry me, please?"

"Yes."

He slipped the ring, a simple round solitaire over her finger and kissed the tips.

"I have to say I never thought you'd propose to me for the second time naked with an erection."

"You thought there'd be a second time?"

"I'm half Italian."

He laughed and scooped her into his arms. "Let's go explore that passionate Italian side then."

Racing up the stairs, he'd never been happier and knowing what their future held only made him more excited for it.

EPILOGUE

"Thank you for doing this, I know it will mean a lot to Nadia."

Gideon shook Jack's hand as they waited at the end of the aisle in Mr Johnson's now-converted barn. As soon as the word got out that he and Nadia were getting married, offers had flooded in to help them. He'd been touched by how this community had accepted a stranger, and not just the Shadow team but the people of this village.

"Wouldn't have missed it for the world. Duchess means a lot to us all."

Gideon glanced at the people who were waiting to celebrate with them. Jack's wife, Astrid, with her infant son in her arms, was seated beside Alex and his wife and daughter. Zack and Ava were with their two children, Riley and Ella. Miss Rose and her daughter were grinning at him from the second row. Charlie was beside Bishop, who held his six-week-old daughter Iris in his arms.

Gideon felt a pang in his gut of want. He wanted that with Nadia and today was the start. Music began to play and Lotus and Aoife stepped into view. The two women were acting as her bridesmaids. They looked lovely in olive green gowns, but his eyes were glued to the back of the room, and when Nadia stepped into sight he almost lost it.

Tears hit his eyes, almost blinding him, and he blinked to clear his vision, biting his lip to keep more at bay. A choked sob slipped from his lips and he felt a hand on his shoulder.

"Keep it together, brother."

Gideon nodded as Damon, his best man, kept him from running up the aisle and grabbing her out of the hands of her father.

She looked like a dream he'd never dared to have. Her dress was ivory lace and skimmed her curves, ending in a train that dragged the floor as she floated towards him. He'd never felt more unworthy or more determined to be the man she'd be proud to call husband.

Her father kissed her cheek and handed her over to Gideon. "Look after her."

"I will, sir."

Her hand shook as it was placed in his, and he raised it to his lips and kissed her gently on her palm.

"You look... I have no words."

"You look handsome, too."

"Ladies and gentlemen, we come here today...."

Jack spoke, his speech something Gideon hardly heard, so engrossed in the spell this woman had cast on him so many months ago. He recited his lines and promised to love her until he died and she did the same. He went to slip the ring over her finger and saw new ink on her ring finger.

It was his name tattooed on her skin and he almost blubbered again like a big baby. "Nice ink."

"Thank you. I like it."

She winked as Jack pronounced them husband and wife and, before permission was given, she was in his arms. Everyone but them fell away as he kissed his wife for the very first time. Her tongue slid against his, her breasts pressed against his chest, and he knew he had to pull away or walk back down the aisle with an erection.

Cheers and joy surrounded them and he'd never been happier, although later that night he thought might top that.

～

"I can't believe you're married."

Duchess sat for a second beside Snow and Charlie, who were both nursing their babies. "I can't believe you two have babies."

"My vagina can."

Snow was only two weeks post-partum, her stubborn son coming two weeks late. Elliot was adorable, with his mother's blond hair and his father's piercing eyes. Iris, Charlie and Bishop's rainbow baby, was all her mother, from her hair to her eyes, and her father was besotted.

"So you and Gideon next?"

Duchess laughed and went to answer, but Miss Rose who'd appeared from nowhere beat her to it. "Not yet, deary. Her twins won't be along until the year after next."

"Twins?"

"Oh yes, dear, you're a double yolker."

"I'm a what?"

Rose's daughter rushed up and took her mother's arm and gently led her away. "Come on, Mum. Let's not upset the bride on her wedding day."

"Pfft, she should be excited. Giddy-up was."

Duchess looked at Snow and Charlie and they all burst out laughing.

"Oh my God, I'm not sure which is funnier, her calling Gideon Giddy-up and him letting her or the thought of you having twins."

"Stop, we're not having twins."

"You sure? She was bang on the money about me and Noah."

Duchess held up a finger. "Don't even say it."

Leaving the two mothers, she went to find her husband and saw him standing with Jack and Bás at the bar. His eyes found her as if he'd been looking and he held his arm out for her. She leaned into his side, her hands moving under his jacket, and she could feel the warmth of his skin.

"Champagne?"

"Yes, please."

She took a sip and then looked up at her husband. She'd never get tired of that word. "So, I had an interesting conversation with Miss Rose."

"Oh?"

"Yeah, she informed me twins are in our future."

"She told me that, too."

"This doesn't scare you?"

Gideon kissed her temple, and she closed her eyes to soak in the tenderness. "Not even a little bit."

Jack laughed "It's only an old lady guessing, anyway."

Bás shook his head. "No, she's been right about every single prediction so far."

Jack paled and placed his drink on the bar. "Excuse me for a sec."

Duchess watched him rush over to where Miss Rose was talking to Astrid and laughed.

"Never thought I'd see the day when a five-foot grandmother would frighten Jack Granger."

"Me either but the planets must have aligned somewhere."

Duchess felt her husband's hand caress the skin of her back where the dress lay low, and shivered with desire.

She tried to concentrate on Bás. "So, no Val. When is she back?"

Bás frowned his features turning dark. "Not sure. Excuse me."

He walked away and Gideon moved her to face him. "Smooth."

She grinned and cocked her head. "I have my moments."

"Yeah?"

She went on tiptoes and wrapped her arms around his neck, her lips brushing his ear. "Yeah."

His thumbs swept over her hips as he held her against his hard cock. "Prove it."

"I'm not wearing underwear."

Before she could react she was over Gideon's shoulder and he was carrying her toward the exit. Her laughter as he rushed out of the barn and into the cold night drowned out the delighted gasps of the guests.

"Gideon, people will know."

"Don't care."

She didn't much care either. Being with Gideon had gifted her a freedom she hadn't felt before to stop being the pleaser and do things for herself.

He set her down in a stable, a horse whinnied close by, the only light a dim one from the office lamp. "In here."

He pulled her toward the office and kissed her as he walked with her, his tongue twining with hers, his hands skimming her long skirt up her thighs until he touched her skin. "So fucking soft."

"I need you, Gideon."

Her hands moved to his belt and she knew this would be quick for both of them. She was already on the edge and as her thumb swept over the pre-cum on his weeping cock she knew he was too.

"Turn around."

His voice was a rasp in her ear as he spun her, his hand on her hips and then he was caressing the skin of her bare ass. His hand swatted and she yelped before the feel of his mouth over her pussy turned it to a whimper of pleasure.

"Oh."

"Teasing me when I could've had this pussy earlier."

His tongue lapped at her slit, his lips closing over her clit as he shoved her closer and closer to her climax. His finger at her ass made her tense and he swatted her again.

"Keep still and let me love my wife."

Her insides melted at his words as he probed her ass with his thumb and then dipped his head again to her clit.

When her orgasm hit she cried out, her pussy clenching emptily but not for long. Before she could even come down Gideon thrust inside her, giving her what she needed most—him.

"Fuck, you're perfect." He palmed her breast over the lace of her gown and pinched. "I can't wait to get my mouth on these tits."

"Gideon, I'm close."

His thrust sped up as he angled his hips, bending his knees as he fucked her over a desk in a stable. Unintelligible sounds burst from her lips as her climax hit, taking her legs from her as she sagged and Gideon roared his pleasure into her neck, his come inside her igniting another tremor of pleasure to ripple through her.

"I love you, Cookie."

He kissed her, his head angled as he pulsed inside her still, and she sighed in utter contentment.

She'd never been happier than in this moment and she knew it was just the start for her and Gideon, and couldn't wait for what the future held, be that twins, triplets, or more.

∼

This might be the happy ever after for Duchess and Gideon, but for a sneak peek of Bás and Val's story, read on.

SNEAK PEEK: FIGHTING SALVATION

"Bás, you have a visitor."

Pushing the papers aside, he sighed. He didn't have the time or patience for visitors. "Send whoever it is in, Titan."

Bás stood and shock registered on his face when he saw Jack and Rafe walk through the door of his office. "Jack, what are you doing here?" He shook both men's hands and clocked the grim expression on Rafe's face. He and Val were brother and sister and looked a lot alike. Thinking of Val made things worse. Only he'd be fool enough to fall in love with a woman he could never have, and worse, for her to feel the same.

"We have a problem and if you don't fix it, I'm going to break every bone in your body."

Bás cocked his head at the threat from Rafe.

"That's enough, Rafe."

"Will someone tell me that fuck is going on here?"

"Val is missing."

His chest felt like it had closed up, the air in his lungs trapped, his belly dipped, and he thought he might puke. "What?"

"She usually checks in with me or Nix every day but for the past two, it's been radio silence. I've tried to call her, even called the place she's staying, and nobody has seen her."

"Hang on." Bás rushed around his desk, his destination the tech room. He felt Rafe and Jack on his heels but his focus was exact. "Watchdog, tell me where Val is right this second."

Watchdog held back his usual desire to spout facts as if sensing the seriousness of the situation. His fingers flew over the keyboard, and screens began to flash on the monitors.

"Shit."

"Talk to me, Watchdog."

Bás hands fisted, and he thought he might explode if he didn't get the information he needed immediately. Panic was a useless emotion and one he'd learned to control years ago but now it was edging across his vision like a snake about to strike.

"It's showing she's still in Germany but when I checked the time stamps, she hasn't moved for two days."

"So the tracker is there but she isn't?"

"Unless she's sick or just staying inside the cabin."

"Does it show her walking Monty or Scout?"

Watchdog pressed some buttons and shook his head. "No."

"Fuck."

"If anything happens to my sister, you're a dead man."

Bás turned to Rafe, who was glaring at him with a fierce promise in his eyes. He didn't say it but if anything had happened to Valentina, he wouldn't have to, Bás would do it himself. "I'll find her."

"You'd better."

"Watchdog, call the team in now."

"We want to help. Valentina is one of us, too."

Bás considered Jack's request and knew it wasn't really a request at all. "You know this is probably Hansen."

Jack's jaw hardened. "All the more reason."

"Then let's do it."

Before he could set a foot outside the room, his phone rang and a chill went down his spine at the unknown number. Usually, he wouldn't answer but he knew he had to, even though everything in him shied away from it. "Yes?"

"You should really take better care with your belongings, Bás. A pretty thing like her could get hurt, or worse."

His gut rolled, his vision blurring with the fury and impotent anger burning through him. "Hansen, if you touch a hair on her head I'll gut you like a pig."

"Now, now temper, Bás. It will get you in trouble one day."

"Where is she?"

He ignored the way Rafe fought Jack to get to the phone in his hand and turned his back, his sole focus on the man he despised.

"Safe for now, although she's quite the wild cat. I like that in a woman."

"You keep your filthy hands off her."

"I'll be in touch."

The phone went dead in his hand and he threw it across the room, a roar exploding from his throat. This was war.

WANT A FREE SHORT STORY?

Sign up for Maddie's Newsletter using the link below and receive a free copy of the short story, Fortis: Where it all Began.

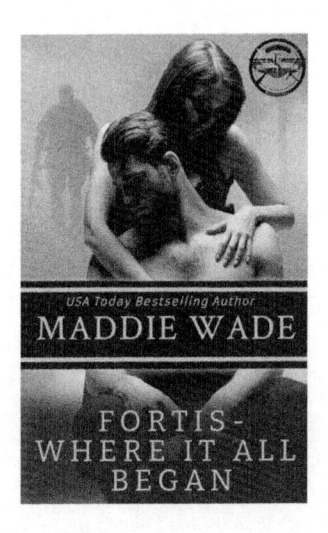

When hard-nosed SAS operator, Zack Cunningham is forced to work a mission with the fiery daughter of the American General, sparks fly. As those heated looks turn into scorching hot stolen kisses, a forbidden love affair begins that neither had expected.

Just as life is looking perfect disaster strikes and Ava Drake is left wondering if she will ever see the man she loves again.

https://dl.bookfunnel.com/cyrjtv3tta

BOOKS BY MADDIE WADE

FORTIS SECURITY

Healing Danger (Dane and Lauren)

Stolen Dreams (Nate and Skye)

Love Divided (Jace and Lucy)

Secret Redemption (Zack and Ava)

Broken Butterfly (Zin and Celeste)

Arctic Fire (Kanan and Roz)

Phoenix Rising (Daniel and Megan)

Nate & Skye Wedding Novella

Digital Desire (Will and Aubrey)

Paradise Ties: A Fortis Wedding Novella (Jace and Lucy & Dane and Lauren)

Wounded Hearts (Drew and Mara)

Scarred Sunrise (Smithy and Lizzie)

Zin and Celeste: A Fortis Family Christmas

Fortis Boxset 1 (Books 1-3)

Fortis Boxset 2 (Books 4-7.5

EIDOLON

Alex

Blake

Reid

Liam

Mitch

Gunner

Waggs

Jack

Lopez

Decker

~

SHADOW ELITE

Guarding Salvation

Innocent Salvation

Royal Salvation

Stolen Salvation

Lethal Salvation

Fighting Salvation

~

WOMEN OF DECEPTION (ZENOBI)

Palace of Betrayal (September 2022)

~

ALLIANCE AGENCY SERIES (CO-WRITTEN WITH INDIA KELLS)

Deadly Alliance

Knight Watch

Hidden Obsession

Lethal Justice

Innocent Target

Power Play

Until Forever (Shane and Emme Wedding Novella)

~

RYOSHI DELTA (PART OF SUSAN STOKER'S POLICE AND FIRE: OPERATION ALPHA WORLD)

Condor's Vow

Sandstorm's Promise

Hawk's Honor

Omega's Oath

Lyric's Truth

~

TIGHTROPE DUET

Tightrope One

Tightrope Two

~

ANGELS OF THE TRIAD

01 Sariel

∼

OTHER WORLDS

Keeping Her Secrets *Suspenseful Seduction World* (Samantha A. Cole's World)

Finding English P*olice and Fire: Operation Alpha* (Susan Stoker's world)

About the Author

Contact Me

If stalking an author is your thing and I sure hope it is then here are the links to my social media pages.

If you prefer your stalking to be more intimate, then my group Maddie's Minxes will welcome you with open arms.

General Email: info.maddiewade@gmail.com
Email: maddie@maddiewadeauthor.co.uk
Website: http://www.maddiewadeauthor.co.uk
Facebook page: https://www.facebook.com/maddieuk/
Facebook group: https://www.facebook.com/groups/546325035557882/
Goodreads: https://www.goodreads.com/author/show/14854265.Maddie_Wade
Bookbub: https://partners.bookbub.com/authors/3711690/edit
Twitter: @mwadeauthor
Pinterest: @maddie_wade
Instagram: Maddie Author